JUST NOD IF YOU CAN HEAR ME

JUST NOD IF YOU CAN HEAR ME

Just
Nod
If You
Can
Hear Me

Just
Rae Elle Riley

TABLE OF CONTENTS

Early Quit

DEDICATION

The following is presented
as fiction. Any similarities
to events real or fabricated
are purely coincidental.

Everything in here is for Michelle. It's all for her.

Job-Safety Analysis

A WORD FROM THE PRESIDENT...

Life is weird, brothers and sisters. I've been riding out thirty-four years of *weird* with all the chop and white water that goes with it, and so I'm writing this to you now as a warning: I don't know what's beyond this next bend up ahead, but it sure sounds loud.

You see, I've snapped, my friends. Not that snapping is really an impediment in our industry: it's more of a polishing agent than anything else, some character quality of blended swagger and eccentricity that works itself through the sinew and sanity of mushy apprentices and somewhere, at some time, in those chosen, it takes root and bubbles out from bellies positioned just over the outer latitude of their belt buckles, then up their spines of fused vertebrae, and finally fans out into these great, wide backs of knuckling muscle that make the evolved fitter both monstrous and maybe even a little top-heavy.

Now, I'm not talking about the sort of snapped that encroaches the mind around the back nine of a seven-twelves job. Or the kind of madness only a welder knows when he finds out the reason the root keeps sugaring up on that smallbore stainless line running three-quarters of an inch off the ground is because his four-hundred-pound out-of-town fire watch has been standing with shifting gait on his internal purge line since before the tacks. No, not the kind of reasonable madness that has you charting the logistics of killing and dismantling a four-hundred-pound man.

I mean the kind of snapped that has you do *really* crazy shit. Like whatever the hell this is.

I love this job. How can you not love it? Especially at first, with youth and vigor at your back. And *especially* against the backdrop of whatever it was you called yourself prior to your proper title: Steamfitter. After a few years, you can't believe the honest world works the way it does. With its salaries and softened tongues, and slacks, and clean interiors, most of us would burst with boredom after knowing life can be lassoed a football field above the city in a man-basket with a partner who calls out most Mondays. Or tunneled through, twenty feet under a trolley track in a partially shut down five-way intersection bisecting a crumbling southwest sector of corner boys and a budding neighborhood of frontline, ghetto queers.

Life doesn't have to go the way it's supposed to. In fact, I have a working theory: Its deviations are intentional, and the more we dredge the channels most highly trafficked, the more we get lost in the suck back of displaced sediment and drift down a leg of river that runs decidedly shallower than anticipated. And so, here I stand. Knee deep in the shallows with dry-rot, American-made, lace-up boots. And I'm starting to feel the wet get into my socks. I guess I just got to say it.

I'm transgender. Or something of it, aiming roughly at some womanly end I can't quite envision but happy enough to live out an existence maybe more truly defined as non-binary. The point is: I'm the first transgender union steamfitter I've ever heard of, both in our territory and beyond. And whether you agree with what I've done or not, you can see why someone in this particular circumstance, be it sane or snapped, would hesitate to invite the bulk of the local to barge in, sullied and savage, into one's most intimate and sterile secret.

But time is a-ticking, brothers and sisters. I can't sit in limbo any longer. And so, I've snapped and invited this new guest to our meeting tonight. Now I'd like to introduce every poor, trapped, blue-collared bastard in transition, blockaded between the ball busting of whatever job they're on and a voice in their mind that never relents a rhetoric of exceedingly hateful self-talk. Sad truth is some of them are already here. Scattered throughout the lot of us, they are an incognito bunch, as equally fat, or drunk, or dead as any other. And if I had to guess as to why you haven't seen a more glittery array of bedazzled trans sycophants dangling from an I-beam on the last construction site you were on, it might be that this shit is hard. I mean, we all know this shit is hard. Up, down, straight athlete: this job is hard. Union trades are hard work. It's why we like them, somewhere, deep down. And the money. That helps too. But it's hard, physical work that requires a thick, leathery disposition that betrays not one watery moment of weakness against the oftentimes endless physical and verbal barrage. And even as I write it, I wouldn't change it. One of God's last natural running filters that churns the weak out with the flotsam and leaves the strong to settle in the brine as some new brackish thing too dense to dissolve. And it's a beautiful, nasty toughness this career creates. One that neither *despair, nor weariness nor endless barren miles could subdue.*[1]

And I'm not writing this to change any of that. Rest assured, my more arrogant reader, nothing of this is to encourage a softer, gentler workplace, teeming with sensitivity and proper pronoun usage. But I will say, if you're out there, *you*, the one I'm really speaking to: I get it. I've wailed, face down on my basement concrete, trying to push my head through the floor. Dear Lord, do I get it. And so, I'm writing this for you, my double agents the world over. This is my signal against everything else that looks like fire.

To the trans, the twisted, the closeted, and the dead, I write this for you. To every poor soul killing themselves *normal* with booze and drugs, happy to bypass their idle hours in chemically induced stupor rather than fight the phalanx of mounting forces in the mind. And especially to all those torn in two. Ripped between a career they love and an identity they've tried to delete, but just won't go away. I'm not here saying I can fix it, but I get it, and I'm with you, and I'm still alive, so just hold on.

---

1   I took that line from Tolkien's Return of the King and recited it as a mantra for so much of my adult life it inked into my immortal soul, so fucking sue me why don't ya!

Because I don't know any other way.

For everyone else reading this, you must know that there are explicit instructions for when I die. They're to pry open, if they can, that ancient half-pint of my father's 1980s shellac in the basement and paint-roller whatever's left of it over my naked form, lying arm up over my head, finger forward, Superman-style. Then tie an American flag cape around my back and trebuchet what's left of me, end over end, straight over the farthest horizon and out into Earth's orbit, where I can tumble above the planet for as long as it exists, the guardian angel of all those in great escape or fools' gambit. My gravestone epitaph will be scraped or crayoned into stone by whatever means is most convenient at the time and the stone slung, sidearm, straight into the woods, or pitched out the passenger window of a Pontiac at high speed, or used as a wheel chock for the wintering of old boats: it doesn't matter really because the words on that stone will reach exactly who they are meant to reach at the time at which they are meant to reach them. And when they do, they'll forget it all as soon it's read but feel in them maybe some extra throttle on the ride home, and run the late yellow straight through the red and disrupt forever the flow of traffic all the days of the rest of their lives. Unless I think of something better, those words will read, "I did whatever the hell I wanted to in life, and you can too!"

Now I warn you, my younger, more naïve reader. This credo is NOT one of the 48 laws of power, nor is it a habit of highly effective people. It advocates neither thinking, growing, nor enriching anything, especially not your bank account. It is a mantra of how to wound friends and irritate people. Really though, it's nothing more than a trigger phrase for the me in you to hear, a light electrical stimulus, just enough to flake whatever calcification formed on that gland in the brain that houses the beautiful maniac in all of us, and reanimate this immortal spirit that runs the course of all human history and spits back in the face of all insufferable tenets force-fed us since the days of our births. It probably won't give you money, or fame, or love. But this I promise you: if it all falls apart, your life that is, alone in your vehicle, you'll twist the dial off in the damn eleven position on your speakers, and shatter the sleepy verdicts of all those who share proximity to the great booming riff of your soul. And when the song ends, there in the silence, you'll make a sound only bandits know, laughing their way to a good hanging just over the next ridge. That sound you hear is one of the manifestations of freedom. It costs a great deal to win these small moments, but it is a sound you will never forget all the days of your life, and it just may change you permanently.

That's about the best I can hope for. And with any skill, I'll be back with the bulk of these bastards, broker than I was before, gayer (or maybe less gay depending on who you ask), and bleeding, and bashing, and bullshitting our way to retirement with four thousand new opinions about me: good, bad or otherwise.

As for the stories I tell, just know none of it is to disparage this great local of mine. I'll try not to name it, but anyone savvy enough will figure it out. Plus then, after a while, I just got lazy about it. I've changed names and places and some things, but otherwise, whether you agree with my telling it or not, this is how it is. This is the life of a Union Steamfitter. For all its glory and its grit, this is pretty damn true.

So don't get up. You don't have to raise your hand or post something online. I get it, my trapped friends, the atmosphere between a rock and a hard place is too dense, so save your breath. Just nod if you can hear me. And hold on. And maybe I can show you what happens next?

Seven O'clock Start

CHAPTER 1

WHEN DID FRIDAYS STOP BEING ABOUT THE MEN?

Dear God did I have to pee. I was slugging water back out of a twenty-ounce coffee cup I'd scavenged from my car and trying my best not to crack under the unflinching scrutiny of Chloe, the dark skinned, freckle-faced gatekeeper, who kept trying to look inside of me like she could catch glimpses of my soul through hesitant breaks in eye contact. And all the while, I'm cursing myself, and God, and maybe Mitch for two bingers two weeks prior with some Astoria *bitches* we fumbled on just inches from the endzone. And now it's now, and I'm chaffed, and pissing clear into a cup under the menacing glare of Styx's own Charon, who snatches the shaky vial to seal and send off to someone further up Hell's ladder.

"First time Down River?" It was a voice from behind me. "Tom Deopard," he said, and he offered a burnt and calloused mitt with his greeting. "Like leopard with a big 'D.'"

"Chuck Keiran," I said, and I shook his hand. "First Job."

"First job, first period?" His eyes widening like the hopeful cast of a fisherman trolling tried and tested waters.

"Yeah?" I think I said it like a question, and that was enough of a flinch for any seasoned journeyman to pull up on the reel and hook for himself the freshest of fresh fish to bring back to the trailer and to the men.

"Oh, that's great," he said, and he looked me up and down in fanged salivation. I'm pretty sure I still had my shirt tucked in.

We were both hiring on for a railcar job Down River, as it was said, working for a subsectioned-off polypropylene plant attached to what was once the greater real estate of a refinery now in the process of turning natural gas storage facility. Somewhere in that wasteland was an electric company too. But right now, we were sitting on a stoop outside of Chloe's blockhouse waiting for the foreman to grab us.

"Yup. I just bought my fitter mansion. Northeast, three hundred thousand. Yup, I made it, kid."

I couldn't comprehend three hundred-thousand-dollar homes, not at that time, not as a twenty-three-year-old former reverse mortgage salesman with less than half a head on his shoulders, a hollow leg turning into a real problem, and a three-digit checking account. I didn't even really know what benefits felt like. Actually, to be honest, by this point, I still didn't really even know what a steamfitter did.

"Weld, dude," he told me. "Be a fucking welder, dude, and you'll never miss a minute of time... unless you want to. Even if you can't fucking weld it, stainless or some weird alloy, just tell them you can. And then go up the hall every night and practice your ass off and pass the test."

And honestly, that's *exactly* what I did with my career. And this was the greatest advice I ever got in this business by the literal first guy I met.

The foreman was a short, dense hobgoblin of a man. Even more hideous unobstructed by his hard hat and all the rest of his personal protective accoutrements. The worst part, even despite the PPE, hell, even if his whole head was sufficiently bagged and dipped in a bucket of wet cement and left to harden, I'd still have to look at a thumbnail of his unadorned cranium from his gate badge left dangling from the rearview and bouncing off the dash like the trading card of the ugliest man to ever play the game. He couldn't help hiding his contempt for my prep school background.

"What did your parents do?" He asks me this like it's my fault.

"Nurse and a cop," I tell him.

"So you know what it's worth then?"

"What?"

"Your rich kid education."

I sort of thought it was ironic that between this man's income and lineage, his children would have unspoken advantages in this union far beyond what I could hope for at that early stage. That in one year's time, between the truck and the gas card, he made more than my father did in three years. But I just agreed with him. That I was a big, pussy, bag of shit like the rest of my generation, but perhaps with hard work, good behavior, and proper recital of the ethics and attitudes of a true tradesmen I could redeem my plushy soul.

He didn't seem convinced. Nor was I. The foreman was Conrad Stucker. A legend of his own fabrication. After nine years in, I can count on one hand the number of true scrotal skinbags in this business. Conman is the thumb.

Firewatch. The Rorschach Test of the local. Reserved for the old, the green, and the aggressively lazy. It is a duty that seasoned vets should shudder at. And yet some won't crawl out of their shell for anything more. Alone for minutes or maybe even months, in your head and with your thoughts, armed with a fire bottle and a high visibility vest that screams even to the unfamiliar: *dingbat.* And that's where Conman stuck me for sixty hours a week. Standing in a field of modified stone watching weld spatter rain from the rack like molten globs of some fire god's spit chaw. I don't even think I touched a pipe wrench. After a few weeks of that, I wanted to quit. And go back to what?

A month before, I'd be drunk at the reverse mortgage company stuffing fistfuls of lukewarm leads into a briefcase I would later backdoor to my brother's opposing operation, all the while dodging oscillating serves of frantic managerial scalps swatted from wall to wall of the building, shredding anything with typeface on it like the FEDs already had the battering ram gripped up and you could hear their boots marching towards the front door. So, naturally, that was out.

I didn't think my liver or my debt-to-income ratio could handle another degree, even if it came with more financial promise than my current one in English Literature. So, it was the fields of stone and slag for me at that time, and for the best, because after the initial boredom subsided little romantic trickles came into focus of a life significantly *more* than slinging HELOCs to old people and fucking their kids out of an inheritance for a couple grand commission check and to be drunk most workdays.

Now it was early, black dawns and the shriek of severed steam tracing that coiled the product lines like the arterial system of some enormous, unearthed steel behemoth and screamed in the morning night dirty clouds of piss-orange steam that we'd blindly toe through with the start of each day: a motley horde of vibrantly jumpsuit-ed *jitbags*. And before that, a bumpy ride in the bread van, stuffed fifteen or thirty guys deep in transport from the trailers to the jobsite, and the smokers would sit in the back and leave the rear door rolled halfway up and pitch their cigarettes in skillful end over end technique that burst in orange glitter far out in the road behind us, before the gate and outside the expressionless watch of safety.

In the railcar rack still functional behind the one we were newly constructing, tank cars rolled in and out like strings of black pearls to their own unique weighty and pressurized percussion. In stasis, the muffled garble of operators running the length of the rack and rail sending sounds of complicated latching methods and the pursed hiss of trapped product as they unloaded the cars six at a time. Then they'd button the string of them up and a slightly off-sequenced crack of a run of rail couplings would fire first from behind the locomotive and run the whole length of the train until it was rolled away into the indistinguishable cacophony of steel rolling against itself.

And all the while I was taking it in and seeing there was a lot more than just standing around in a field of stone with a hi-vis vest on doing calf stretches to pump feeling back into my feet.

"Chucky, can you do something for me?" It was Deopard. If he asked me to drive a hot rod through my eye, I would have done it just to break the monotony.

"Yeah, whatever you want."

"Fucking Donnie here grabbed me a right-handed pipe wrench. Can you go over by the job box and ask Stucker if we have any lefties?"

And I did it. Yes, your less than humble narrator stared his foreman straight in the eyes and with the confidence and latent energy of a towel boy given the last two minutes of play in an already long since ruined season, I asked a grown-ass man for a left-handed pipe wrench.

"What?" He was handsomer covered in shit. He didn't even chuckle. He walked me back to the men like I was a kid who had wandered too far from the baby pool.

"What the fuck are yous doing?" Stucker said to them, or something equally as boring. Then he launched into a diatribe about fucking around and being behind schedule and all the other things he prioritized over job morale. If that job had been any longer, we might have seen a mutiny.

After he stamped off, Donnie McCutchin told me, "Uh, it's like the military, kid. You don't have to respect the man, but I guess you have to respect the position." And they all went back to work. There were six silent hours left in the day.

Sometime after they laid everybody off, and it was just Conrad and me left, well, he was almost capable of displaying real live human characteristics.

"Yo, Con, I heard a joke on the radio. What's the worst thing someone can hear after giving Willie Nelson a blow job?" He looks up from whatever thought he was lost in and really thinks about it.

"I don't know, what?"

"I'm not Willie Nelson." And he laughed. A real human laugh too. I think I got laid off later that day.

--- - --- - --- - --- - --- - --- - --- - --- - --- - --- - --- - --- - --- - --- - --- - --- - --- - ---

"You got a girlfriend, bud?" It's Vince Kohler and it's another nameless day.

"Garage kept," he would say. "Like the toilet company,

taking shit for just as long, but not nearly as well paid." Did all these guys come with a tagline?

"Yeah, I got a girlfriend," I tell him.

"Let's see a picture." A few others overhear and come lurching towards us like the reborn dead just caught sight of a freshly cracked skull of brains. So I just reach into my pocket and start scrolling through my phone looking for a good one, when Young Teddy Burrows nearly swats me in the back of the head.

"What the fuck are you doing, dawg? NEVER show a fitter your old lady." I lock my phone and look around me. Some of them are on the balls of their feet like a pack of bloodhounds and my nudie pics are the strangled goose.

"These dudes will bang the balls off your old lady and you'll be working twelves on night shift high-fiving the same motherfucker who did it as you pass each other at the gate in the morning. All the while you're snuggling into a stink in your bed you can't quite put your finger on. Trust me. It happens. And if I didn't think you were a homo, I'd bang your old lady too." They called Young Teddy "Wide Nine" because his eyeballs were spaced at least nine inches apart, or so the men speculated. I think he'd kill you if you tried to actually measure it.

"Thank you, Ted," I tell him. "That means a lot." He was the only other apprentice on the job even though he was almost *out of his time* and although he could be a little far-fetched braggadocio, I liked the dude, and figured most of his bullshit was real. And I took that advice to heart, and never let many fitters get too close of a look at *my* old lady.

And those were the days. Boredom and bullshit. Somewhere in all that, something was happening though. That early week awkwardness was dissolving. I was learning my audience—the jokes and rhythms and patois of the bandit horde. And with that came methods of camouflage, and conduct, and even proper retaliation: a perpetually bipolar display of personalities that will leave the incompetent prickly or the pros shining in maniacal revelry. As the years went on, I would realize all of that would file down to this one general truth. The first law of physics in the science of this new world. And that was: **you didn't do this shit unless**

you were nuts. Throughout the years, it would be the *normal* ones who would scare me the most.

Fridays have a weird energy in this business. Days of hype or hindrance and nothing in between. Either you were hurting from last night, pissed off about working the weekend, or drooling like a chained mutt for that first weekend beer and a chance to sleep in. We were working the weekend, and I was hungover as all hell, using the usual methods of reanimation: Red Bull and Marlboro cigarettes. And after pouring about a cup and a half of liquid hot brown out of my ass and onto the frozen stew of shit and blue-black john water that steamed up through my legs like a cloud of mustard gas, I step out back into the normal, breathable atmosphere of that crisp fall dawn and try to refocus my eyes.

"You good, bro?" It's Young Teddy. I light a cigarette and reach for a half-slugged can of Red Bull resting on the bumper of the bread van.

"My first tell, bro. You see me drinking Red Bull and smoking cigarettes, you can rest assured the breathalyzer is going to be a stiff hurdle to navigate." He laughs.

"You smoke weed?" he asks.

"I guess not anymore. They test us like lab rats, right?"

"Stop. You think that dude can pass a piss test?" He gestures to an insulator still sitting in his vehicle with the engine and radio off, not reading or on his phone, but staring blankly ahead like the thoughts in his skull just walked off somewhere and left the body behind. We can't stop laughing.

"I figured where there's a will there's a way," I tell him.

"There's a way," he says, and I think I make my first friend.

Then it's 6:35 and Cholly, the steward and driver of the bread van, is asleep on the floor behind a fold-up table when Conman kicks the door in to the trailer and proceeds to badger and belittle this broken band of beaten bastards like he expects us to jog the mile and a half trip to the jobsite in perfect formation and cadence too. I don't even think Bumpy latched his perpetually agape jaw. But it was enough to wake Cholly up. And so reluctantly and at his own pace, Cholly went out and started the truck, scuffing the heels of his boots the whole way there.

Eventually we moseyed out, the biggest suck pumps first.

Looking back, Larry Grossman was probably going through a bad one on that job. His back was completely destroyed and whatever he was doing during his extracurricular hours made him bitter and raw. He had wet, unsymmetrical, night crawler lips and at that time his face was somewhat pocked up. He also possessed a very common trait of fitter fathers of daughters, where this tug-of-war would occur between the natural urge to regurgitate every prideful boost of his daughter's success and the reluctance to tell any of it to a *fucking scumbag fitter*. It's actually sort of a beautiful thing. Pride almost always wins, and they can't help but tell you *something* about this gem in their lives that sparkles against all the other shit.

But on this particular Friday, there in the back of the bread van, in that blue and pink dawn of smeared orange sunrise, something mean was worming around in Lar's skull. Smoking a Newport 100 he'd bummed from Young Teddy, Larry stepped down off the van, one thick, ramshackle leg at a time, and badged through the gate, still smoking; now on the process side of the plant and re-situated himself back in his seat in the van. His cigarette never betraying the corner of his lips where the two night crawlers met.

Cholly drives. And Lar smokes. And the men start to notice.

"Yo Lar!" Cholly looks at him through the rearview mirror. "You might want to throw that cigarette out."

Larry just sighs, takes one last big drag, and shoots the still-lit thing into a unit we pass on the right. Everyone's eyes just kind of go wide for a second. Then he says in the tone of a true fitter, "When did Fridays stop being about the men?!" And the whole van erupts in laughter, and we forget that the unit behind us could explode to smithereens at any second or maybe never. And I remember in that moment thinking about Henry the Fifth's St. Crispin's Day speech—*We happy few*—and all that. But we had arrived. And there was no time for that now.

Walking across the unit to the railcar job, I think it was me, Bumpy, the Hitman, and Bodybag Bennett. Wide Nine and Lurch were trailing us, and I think GQ was floating around that mix too, but then again GQ had been floating around for years and who knows the last time he made steady contact with sanity or earth soil. I was just a pimple amongst these legends, and I could not help but to interrupt Bodybag the first time I heard the Orangutan story.

"I was there, dude!" Bruce (Bodybag's God-given and subsequently Godforsaken name) was a thick little sparkplug who spoke twice as fast as a normal man, maybe to make up for his diminutive stature.

"This fucking story..." Bumpy could have been thirty or sixty; there was no definitive way to measure his age other than to take the man's word for it, which was unreliable. I suppose you could always cut him in half and count the rings. He was the product of a perpetually long and rough paper route that during the bad times would have the creature polishing off a fifth of Jack Daniel's Tennessee Whiskey every night, and from the bottle. Now he claimed he didn't drink and stayed up most nights restless, watching movies. But the lifestyle had left his skin ragged and dry-aged like a hammered off hunk of crumbly cheese rind. And although today he was sour, I would notice over the years, as I heard this story recounted time and again throughout my career, that in its telling had the power to bring out that reminiscent good-natured quality in men.

In years to come, the orangutan story would always be pitched as the final trump in any contest of big guy stories. And that's because Jack Granger was the quintessential "big guy" for all ages.

"So, Jack's fucking up this monkey, right?" Bodybag continues. "I don't know if I was ever so drunk in my life. Three minutes, three rounds. It was a couple G's or something, and for the first two rounds, I'm telling you dude, he's beating the shit out of this monkey."

And then I can't take it anymore, I have to know.

"Wait. Like a *monkey* monkey?" I interrupt. For the record, it's not proper practice for a first period apprentice to interrupt a journeyman on any subject matter other than to prevent the journeyman's near immediate death, and even then, you'd better be sure about it.

"A gorilla," Bumpy groans.

"No, it was a fucking orangutan! And, kid, you ever hear the expression 'seen not heard?'"

I nod back at Bodybag and make a mental note of the protocol.

"Dude. We're in a Connex box in Atlantic City fighting a monkey for money," Bodybag tries to go on, but now the men are involved in the retelling.

Hitman is old. Like, too old to have to be still working old, but he looks at me and he clarifies, "Jack Granger was an old enforcer for the local."

"And the Pagans," Cholly chimes in.

"And he was special forces paratrooper for the Air Force during the Vietnam war," Bodybag says. "He was like six five, six six, two fifty, solid bone and muscle."

"He was a gentleman, Chucky," Hitman tells me.

"Dude. He missed a weekend of overtime because he stabbed three dudes in the alley behind his house because they were talking too loud and keeping him up, and he only warns people once. He'd give you the fucking shirt off his back though. He was a good guy." And then I realize they're telling the story again because he'd just died the night before. I would come to learn guys in this business didn't get that somber about death. It was something you had to prepare yourself for every day, until you didn't, and then it was just the unconscious inevitable conclusion of life, and there's something philosophical to be said about this psychological reaction that no true fitter could phrase as anything more than: *Who gives a fuck?*

"So, to get the money, you had to do all three rounds, right?" Bodybag takes the spotlight again. "And for TWO ROUNDS, he's fucking this thing up, dude. Then in the third round, this dude, this...monkey trainer or whatever the hell he was, blows this fucking whistle. The orangutan proceeds to grab Jack by the wrist with just his thumb and forefinger"—and he acts the scene out on my own wrist and plays the part of the monkey—"and proceeds to whip Jack across this box like a goddamn ragdoll."

With half a smile on his lips, Larry Grossman says, "You know, I saw him like a week after that limping around the job, and I go,

'Yo, Jack what happened?' and with that voice of his he goes, 'I ripped my fucking asshole out!' and just keeps on limping."

And we're crying now, we're laughing so hard.

Conman's ominous shadow emerges from his truck and stands impatiently by the job box. The men see it and shrug. Collectively their courage could multiply tenfold, and not a member of that group flinched forward one second quicker towards the foreman above that slow, Friday amble. And I just walk on. Still laughing and shaking my head at this strange new world where men fight monkeys in shipping containers for money and kicks.

CHAPTER 2

INSOMNIA

One day all I could write was this:

I can't sleep.
I can't fucking sleep.
48 hours awake.
Then I sleep.
If I take some pills,
But I'm trying to be good.
And not take the pills.
But I can't sleep.
And it's splitting me in two.

You know I used to have a prose that would slice your fucking ear off. Frankly, it felt like an innate gift birthed in the bored moments of an otherwise lonely childhood. A music for the musically talentless. A primordial rhythm in the beat and pace of words that twists out tone and texture in all the same harmonious and dissonant properties, not unlike a well-placed modulation of key signature in your favorite song. But those types of gifts come as talent-show tricks, and we all probably have something like it in us, something to kill a slow five minutes with some light razzle dazzle and a "Look what I can do!" But your wizardry will end at that. Sparklers shot from your fingertips and it might get you laid once or twice, but you'll never fastball a lightning bolt from your fist with any force without the risk of mass and acceleration.

It is a great gamble of power, this going forth, not unlike the trail to the tip of Everest. The dead are shrugged off right there, static and brain-dead, powerless and worse yet, left as a monument to humble all those daring enough to venture one step further than your own futile attempt at the summit.

Well then, wall the summit with frozen corpses! Please, I beg you, because those who turn back, shook by dull logic, face a fate far worse than being made a permanent statute to the pig-headed delusion of fools' glory. They return to Earth, enforcers of a magicless mantra: *It Can't Be.* They rally into the rank and file of rigid routine, happy enough to see a couple more cents added to the pension at the next wage negotiation meeting.

Sometimes I think my head froze into that wall of corpses, enamored by the promise of the top of world, as my body hack-sawed the bottom four-fifths of itself out of the ice right there at the "fair enough" point of my throat. Then it stumbled back down the mountain, a horseless headsman, where it hid its naked neck in a hardhat and safety shades for ten years, content enough to bolt and gasket that new dome that comes issued after five in the trades and the completion of an apprenticeship. Now I mean this as no insult to the trades. Nor do I harbor any enormous shame for being lassoed and driven back down the mountain with the bulk of humanity. Statistically, this is what *we* do. We seek the deep sleep offered only to those who know they've got a place to go tomorrow. And when the alarm goes off in the morning, we'll bitch and moan in chorus with everyone else sharing the same ass-branded ego, and wonder there in our truck what the odds are for grabbing the only rotten apple in the bag without catching a single number on our Powerball ticket. There, gripping the steering wheel tight, we'll never even realize how much less anxious we are than if we were still a couple hundred feet from the summit, tonguing our bellies across the ice because our limbs have long since failed us.

The wall of corpses is mortared in limbs and digits. Heads and hands and hearts, slurried together with the ice to form ornate pilasters of macabre ambition. The fingers of fingerstyle guitarists, the rotator cuffs of collegiate pitching arms, the hearts of poets hole-sawed straight through their chest cavity, all of it and more offered in penance for having been so foolish as to attempt a break for the peak. And then, every now and again, you feel it, like a phantom limb, some strange pressure you can't understand, and think *maybe,* here in this new life which knows nothing of the old, *somebody made a break for it back there on the peak.* Maybe it was the help of your quite-literal foothold, but someone vaulted the wall and made one last trudge for the top. *You* used to be someone. Who are you now? Everest still stands. And you still have breath in your chest.

I don't intend to die on the mountain. I seek, like you, the crown of the world. But should the rest of me freeze into the wall of corpses, only a couple hundred feet from the summit, I'll stare ahead, wide-eyed, until the sun explodes or the ice caps melt and me with them, and scratch little terrible poems out into the ice in the staccato intervals between alive and dead.

CHAPTER 3

PIPELINE AND PISS TESTS

When I am inevitably business manager of this local, I will win the election entirely off a three-word slogan I will have stickered on every square inch of this less than fine city: *No Piss Tests*. But until then, every couple of years or so, I'll probably end up hitting you with a story like this...

By now, I'm second period. Our union apprenticeship is broken up into ten periods spread out over five years, where the *lads* and *lasses* earn incremental raises every six months if they can pass the aptitude testing of the previous period. Good behavior and a quality work report are also taken into consideration and can be the final feather of excess load that'll either leave you stranded in the sand atop the freshly fractured back of your formerly trusty Bactrian or riding high over the dune seas, dripping in silk like a damn sultan. In all fairness, the choice is that of the apprentice.

Also, take note. It is very important to refer to any apprentice, be they eighteen or eighty, with any word synonymous with *child*. Kid. Squirt. Sport. Boy. Girl. Lad. Poop. All will do just fine in the breaking down of unfitterly ego. Just be sure that when you do it you plant some new seed of growth, be it vernacular or maybe even mechanical education. Most importantly, try not to smile when *your* kid reminds you about the takeoff in elevation for an FOB eccentric reducer coming off a riser on the side of a vessel, and effortlessly calls you a "ballbag" while he's doing it. Inside you'll be kissing your fingers like a French chef just made a soufflé out of human flesh, but don't let the kid see this. Just say, "Good point. And shut up." And take this silent pride home with you and beat it to death and never let it see the light of day.

So, I'm second period, which is one period before being indentured in the eyes of the local, and that word means a lot of different things, but for the sake of this story it means you start to have rights and are less easily fired than a first- or second-period nitwit. Basically, until you are indentured, the union's reaction to failed tests, be they written, welded, or urinated, is almost certainly near-immediate expulsion from the trade.

That railcar job had long since ended. I was rehired now by a different contractor, eight miles upriver at an oil refinery that would make international news a few years later after an elbow in the hydrofluoric acid unit failed and created a mushroom cloud of fire and debris so large it could be seen across the entire city. It was reported that one lone shipping container flew as far as the adjacent state, which was more than five miles and two rivers away. Miraculously, nobody was killed in the event.

It was winter. I pulled off that nameless branch of side road before the bridge and crossed a terminator between dawn's night and the orange pulse of *refinery sun* like a lunar rover returning from adventures on the dark side. My two-door Mitsubishi scraped along the meteorite-cratered crust of this environment, which is both alien and seemingly without atmosphere. And all of it alight and alive against a steady respiration of fire and spilt steam.

I like the crunch of boots in winter gravel. The walk from the car through the gate to the trailers is a special sort of silence, pregnant and spirited with a chorus of quiet sounds: the snap of permafrost with each heavy footfall forward, the crackle of meaty spines, the sound of breath, both your own and your brother's labored huff beside you, the flick of lighters before the gate, the choked ignition of a lone diesel coughing to life in the cold, and all of this under the steady roar of flare towers that bespeckle the plant like little eyes of Sauron keeping watch over its orcish inhabitants. To the uninitiated, it's a brief chance to ready oneself before the onslaught of the day. A couple-minute stroll through the lash of winter wind is sometimes enough to snap the slack from your lips and shake off whatever exhaustion or hangover you have brought in with you.

Hollis, affectionately called Olly Oops or Oopsy—though maybe never to his face—because of an accident many years prior that resulted in the death of an apprentice, was the general foreman of that maintenance gang and stood a head shorter than everyone else, with these distinctively fucked up lips that looked like maybe he'd tried kissing an uninsulated steam line years before and half his face melted to the pipe. That being said, he was a class act and loyal to his men and actually gave you a heads up if he thought there might be a work reduction later in the week so you could start eyeing other prospects without suffering a week or more layoff. I headed to his trailer first, which housed the foremen, safety, and QC inspectors because I'd gotten drunk the night before and lost my check somewhere between the bar and my girlfriend's apartment.

I opened the door to the trailer, and before I could even speak, he said, "Who is the Marlin?"

I did not know who the Marlin was, but I started to have a funny feeling about my new nickname.

"Huh? I don't know what you're talking about," I told him. And he smiled. It would be the only time I ever saw the man smile.

"Someone named the Marlin found your check and left a voicemail on payroll." He, Wisniewski, and Boogsy, who had already listened to the message, were chuckling now.

Wisniewski, we called Jizniewski, naturally, because he was Hollis's long-time personal friend, and he routinely abused the benefits the friendship came with. Although I still kind of liked him because he had the shortest fuse I ever seen and spoke in this high-pitched falsetto that would screech even higher when his top blew. That, and most of his joints were fused together except for maybe the shoulders and the hips, and so he walked around the plant like a blown-out G.I. Joe straight down to the mustache, which desperately tried to signal he was not a homosexual. Oh, and he had a facial tic that looked like he was in the grips of a light stroke at all hours of the day. It was very difficult not to laugh when he inevitably flipped out that week or day or hour.

"Who the fuck is the Marlin, buddy?" If Wisniewski liked you, you were "buddy." If he hated you, you were "pal." It was another tick in the time bomb of the man's life and career.

"Give me that fucking phone," I said.

"Put it on speaker," Boogsy told me, and he cupped his hands behind his head and drank in my anxiety like it came served in a coconut with a little umbrella dangling out of it.

And there, in that dusty trailer, in the morning, before we shipped out to our respective jobs or hiding places we listened to the deranged lunacy of a kind-hearted maniac as he explained how, why, and where he'd found my paycheck in a parking lot behind my apartment, and left only a phone number and the moniker, Marlin, as a means of contact.

"Are you gonna meet him?" Boogs asked between great heaves of laughter.

"And wake up in a pit putting lotion on my skin?" I didn't think so. *Little did I know at that time, but if anyone was going to be lubing up potential victims and sewing a skintight bodysuit of their shucked epidermis, I was a more likely suspect than the Marlin.* But did I want this maniac holding on to my personal information? At some time, unbeknownst to the men, I called and left a message. And it would be a choice that would haunt me until this day now.

"Let's take it to the other trailer and let the men hear it, buddy!" Jizniew could shatter glass he was so excited.

"Let's," I said, certainly not meaning it.

And just like that, I was the Marlin. Honestly, I breathed a sigh of relief that I got coined a nickname that didn't involve balls or some perpetual reminder of a physical deformity. I wonder what my nickname will be after I publish all this. I assure you, despite its offensiveness, it will be both highly accurate and to the correct audience, hilarious. I hope my knee-jerk is to chuckle the first time I see it written on a shithouse wall with stylized figures accompanying it, labeled in detail from dimensions to alternate views. If I do this right, maybe I'll laugh on all the way to death, which is all I ever really wanted.

After a day of telling and retelling the story a hundred thousand times, I go home and I shower and I eat, and right as my head touches the pillow my phone rings, and the phone says "The Marlin."

"Charles? This is Marlin. I found your check in the parking lot. I will meet you on Main Street. I will be blowing a whistle." And then he hung up, and I don't even know if I spoke, so I just started walking up Main Street because how could I not? And sure as shit, walking down the street blowing a whistle, with a hat on that read MARLIN, I meet the mythical beast face to face.

"You must be my man?" I say reading the hat.

"Charles?" And the Marlin begins to recount the story word for word as it was recorded on that initial voice message. He was a heavyset man with a scraggly beard and eyes that looked somewhat loose in his skull, and he told me how he just woke up from a six-month nap, and that he was allowed to live on his own again. Mostly, he was just a kind madman lonely for a friend. He would remind me every six months for the next eight years via text message that he had found my check in a parking lot. I never responded and just said little prayers when I received the texts. Man was just looking for a friend. I could have done more than God did if I had just sent back a smiley face.

There was a coup against Hollis and his crew, led by the one and only Anthony Lewis. Remember that single hand of steamfitter shit stains I spoke of in the first chapter? Tony was the index finger used to unclog impacted assholes. His flesh emitted a natural lubricant, which allowed him to slither around the plant on his belly, undetected. Worst of all, he could be almost human to your face, and most didn't believe his undeath until they felt the pump of blood down their own neck from two fang marks.

Somehow, and I'll spare you the slimy details, Tony was able to pin an inefficiently run *shutdown* on Hollis, even though Tony was the one running the job and Hollis was occupied with his maintenance crew. For those of you who don't know, a shutdown is the temporary *shutting down* of a unit so that crews can work around the clock to repair, maintain, and install pumps, and pipes, and crackers, and exchangers, all in a sometimes-desperate attempt to get the unit back up and running as quickly as possible. They can be planned years in advance or fired off at the hip from the starter pistol of some rogue operator looking to advance himself in both ladder and reputation. Both are gloriously rotten debacles, but it seems those frantic, unscheduled shutdowns of lofty ambition almost always result in that paradoxically Zen state of suffering known only as *blood money,* where the waking state of your conscious agony *almost* outweighs the weekly deposits to your checking account. Regardless, the rumors were starting to reach as far as the men, which meant Hollis's days were numbered, and subsequently our own by associated allegiance.

Which sucked for me because it was here in this hellhole that I began to really cut my teeth in this business. Cory Kaufman, a fully illustrated biker stoic, was spending every lunch break with me practicing welding down at our "fab shop," which goes against the grain even now to say because it was a palleted shanty town of shipping containers and broken-down tool trailers. It had been placed at the bottom of a hill, stupidly mind you, so that when it rained, rainbow-colored rapids would run under our feet and straight through the shop, and the welders worth their salt would just go home tired of being electrocuted five hundred times a day. Steve Russo and Art Collins were teaching me everything else. Not just the tools and math and work ethic of a proper fitter but also helping me to relax some of those young *kid* jitters that can drive a veteran absolutely insane. And Hollis saw all of this and commented, "That kid doesn't know shit, but he certainly wants it." That was all I could prove at that time. And I took it as a great compliment.

To his credit, Hollis shipped me off. He knew Tony had his own crew of kids, and seeing as I had knowledge of the full history of events, he surely figured I could be a source of future insurrection, and even though I was nobody, I was a loose end destined for the firing squad like everyone else. That day at lunch, he came into the men's trailer and slipped me a note with an address and a phone number on it.

"Kid, go here tomorrow. And call Greg Nash when you get there."

"Thanks." I said, *I think*. I shook his hand, and he left. He would be dusted the following week along with everyone else in the crew, except one or two hangers on, and it doesn't take a master sleuth to figure out who the moles were in that old crew.

Now ... Allow me to take the time to explain a little something about synthetic urine. If you don't order it online, it's sold in sex shops, marketed to those with piss fetishes so out of control yellow food dye just won't cut it. And so, per the instruction of some of my new friends, I went to the recommended sex and smoke shop and purchased the most popular brand of synthetic urine. The man behind the counter looked like some early model of autonomous cyborg, but I certainly wouldn't refer to the tissue surrounding his robotic endoskeleton as *living*.

"Hey, throw one of those big double-enders in there too, while you're at it!" I said it as a joke, but the man didn't flinch and just rung the thing up lifelessly.

"Uh, I was kidding, man. I'll just take the piss and the smokes and the chocolate bar."

If he had said, "Affirmative," I wouldn't have flinched. He pressed one button on his computer, which deleted the eighty-dollar purchase, and placed the big, purple, jiggly thing back in its proper receptacle. I was now the proud owner of one *Get Out of Jail Free Card*, or so I thought.

I take the time to tell you this, my most regal reader, because I know you would never associate yourself with such debauched behavior as to cart around synthetic urine with you all day, masquerading in your lunchbox as a microwavable cup of Campbell's soup. No, never, of course not. But at that time, my alcoholism was in the throes of the marijuana maintenance program, and if I just stuck to drink without a little pot to slow me down some, I could be *really* dangerous. Mind you, I had one rule I actually never broke: I was never high or drunk on the job. It was too dangerous for myself and my friends. Doesn't mean I wasn't good for a callout every now and again.

The day after Hollis slipped me that note, I reported to a tank farm for the same contractor under the same jurisdiction as the client we were working for in the refinery. So I had concluded that I would not have to retest upon arrival, and left my piss cold in my lunch box, and smoked a big fat one the night before. That assessment would prove to be incorrect.

There, in this new trailer back in the woods in the rear of the tank farm, I shook hands with the new cast of characters I would meet on this job and began filling out "new hire" paperwork, which should have been my first indication that something was afoot. There was Gonzo, Hands Duran, Regan, and Randy Falkner. GQ was running the job, and Boogsy was already there working as a "consultant," so he could both collect retirement and continue being paid a lucrative wage in the process, a gray area the union would go back and forth on over the years. Nash was the general foreman. Looks-wise, he was something between Baron Harkonnen and a creature out of *The Hills Have Eyes*, and it was rumored that in his youth he could be a bit of a *beaut*, and by that I don't mean *load*, but I believe the man liked to drink and even more so to smoke. The story went that on the night before his triple bypass surgery he smoked as many cigarettes as his lungs could extinguish before his wife rushed him to the hospital. They said he died on the table a few times. By now, he could barely walk or stand or waddle. An absolute gentleman to me, though.

Then I hear the Louisiana welding inspector, who more often than not had last night's dinner still stuck between his teeth, ask Gonzo if he'd studied for the test, and my heart sunk down into my asshole. As calm as could be feigned, I reached into my cooler, grabbed my cup of piss soup, and tucked it into my sweatshirt pocket without detection. Then I got up and made my way to the port-a-john outside, and this Louisiana boy stopped me and confirmed my deepest fears before I reached the trailer door.

"You know you gonna have to piss in like fifteen minutes, right?"

"No doubt," I told him as I opened the door. "But I'll shit my pants before then. Don't worry. I'll still have to piss." And I shut the door in his face before he could breathe on me again.

In the john, I fumbled with hand warmers and rubber bands and said fifteen Hail Marys in forty-five seconds. I tucked the cold bottle against my gooch in the warm pocket between my balls and b-hole. Back in the trailer, I willed warm energy down into my groin, and misspelled my name and address on my paperwork as the anxiety of losing everything I had worked for became nearly overwhelming. I played up the recent trip to the restroom, and so they let me go last, and by the grace of God and the principles of thermodynamics, my urine was up to temperature by the time I poured it into the vial. I said a quick, "Thank you," to my Nana who had recently passed away and sealed that golden ambrosia of Zeus himself with a signature and a sigh of relief. I think I walked around the rest of the day two inches off of the ground.

That Friday I was off due to my Nana's funeral, and after a shot of whiskey in her honor, my brothers and girlfriend slipped out for a blunt in the car outside. I was literally exhaling my first hit when my phone rang. It was Nash. I told everyone to shut the fuck up.

"Chucky? Now don't worry, but there was something wrong with your drug test."

"Really?" I oversold the reply, but fuck it, I was in this deep.

"Don't worry, it happened to another guy too." And I was just grateful another guy on the job was doing drugs. "So, you'll come in Monday and piss again, ok? Then you got to sit home until the test comes back clean. But I talked to the agents already and you're gonna get paid for your time."

I couldn't care less about that and just said, "That's wonderful." Then he hung up, and I took one last rip of the blunt and told my family I had to go back to that sex shop.

Remember that scene in *A Christmas Story* when Ralphie is daydreaming at the dinner table about the adventures he will inevitably have once he's in possession of his Red Ryder BB gun? Well, it was like that but with a hollowed-out strap-on with built in piss reservoir and battery-operated heating element, and it only came in African American. "Don't worry, Dad. As long as I got Ol' Blue…"

"Two hundred and eighty dollars," the cyborg recited.

"What?!" I'm fairly certain that was more than my entire net worth. Certainly more than my liquid assets. So that was out. And little did I know, that might have been my first experience with divine intervention.

That Sunday, I stayed over with the ONLY friend I knew who could produce clean urine for me on the spot. He shared the apartment with a longtime weirdo friend who left the thermostat at eighty-eight and answered the door wrapped in a towel glistening from sweat in his own place like a fucking McPoyle from *Always Sunny in Philadelphia*.

"Pete likes it hot," my buddy told me.

And so I said, "Gross." And lay on his couch all night awake in sweat and anxiety.

The next morning in the trailer with my buddy's piss in a flip-top perfume bottle tucked into my Under Armor underpants (my personal recommendation for any of you foolish enough to attempt the ol' switcheroo), I sat on a rusty, metal fold-out waiting for someone to determine my fate. Headlights. And the decompression of a heated interior against that frosty morning. The crack of joints and the recognizable sigh and grunt before scaling the steel steps leading up to the trailer. It was Boogsy. Not the Boogeyman of lore some twenty years before, but the evolved, aged Pop Pop of that mythical creature, known now only as Boogs. And thank God it wasn't some jerkoff.

"Hey, kid." He started chuckling when he saw me. "Hey, you know they have to watch you piss, right?"

The life poured out of my face, and I must have turned ghost white. I gave Boogsy a silent look that said this was going to be quite difficult. He read the expression word for word, looked down at the floor, and shook his head ever so slightly. I read it as, "Don't tell *me* about it."

So we waited for the drug test person. I was hoping we would get the same beautiful Latina nurse we had last time, and in my young vanity I thought maybe I could flirt my way out of this situation. Nope. We got king jerkoff. The door to the trailer kicks open and standing there is a squared off hall monitor, too dumb or predictable for the Force, and so now he's a piss boy carrier pigeon by day, caped crusader by night. And I honest to God think the first words out of his mouth were, "Where's the perp?" Oh boy. This was going to be awesome.

He escorts me to a room in the rear of the trailer and as he begins setting up his laptop, he explains to me *how it was going to be*.

"So your test came back inconclusive..." I say nothing and stand with my arms folded behind him.

"Usually an indication of foul play." I try not to roll my eyes and remind him about the other guy on the job walking around with an inconclusive.

"Maybe it's something on your end?" He ignores the question.

"So I'm going to need you to sign this email, then drop your trousers here in this trailer to make sure you are not wearing any apparatus..." *Oh thank God I didn't get my Red Ryder BB Dick for Christmas!* "Then we'll head out to the port-a-john outside, and I'll need to physically watch you urinate in the cup."

This was it. I was fucked. Anxiety, whatever that chemical is composed of in the body, was in full blown reactive explosion now, and I thought I might actually start foaming at the mouth. But just then, I heard a voice. Maybe it was my own, maybe my recently deceased grandmother, maybe it was the Lord Christ himself, but it said very distinctly, *If they're going to catch you, have them catch you the hard way.* And so I committed to that path.

King Jit fiddled with his web browser with his back to me, and I adjusted the bottle between my legs so that my butt cheeks could grip it. Then I leaned in, signed his thing, took one step back, and dropped trou.

"We good, boss?" I said in phony aggravation. He looked at my tackle and nodded. As I pulled my drawers up the bottle fell from my ass and luckily tipped pants-side as it bounced off the rear of my belt. I breathed one nearly inaudible sigh of relief. First hurdle navigated.

As we stepped outside and headed towards the john, I remember thinking, *How the fuck am I going to pull off this next trick?*

Standing there now, facing the man, I reached my hand in first and with the expert sleight of hand only a master magician could recognize, I tucked the bottle under my b-bag and held it against my gooch with nothing more than about my pinky finger. Then I explained to the man, I was not going to be able to urinate with him staring at me. He was unmoved by my pleas.

"Listen. I'm just going to turn to the side and get started, then I'll turn and face you," I tell him.

"Unacceptable."

I do it anyway, and as I turn, I squeeze a few drops of pure golden sweetness into the cup.

"You can't do that," he tells me. I do that. Again and again and again for five of the most awkward minutes of my life, and all the while I'm acting out the theatrics of a child trying to show mommy he really doesn't have to go.

Finally, the bastard relents and says, "How much you got in there?"

"Forty milliliters."

"Ok that's enough." *Wait. What? I did it?*

I follow the man back inside, my hands in the throe of a complete Parkinson's tremor. We sit down at the table, and he passes me two smaller vials and tells me to pour thirty milliliters in one and ten in the other. My hands were shaking so bad I spilled a few drops in the pour and used the last of my sanity and conscious effort to steady them. Once sealed and signed, the man passes me a receipt for my efforts. I 180 my attitude immediately and begin to finally start swinging from these corner ropes I've been up against.

"Yo, so when do you think we'll see the results on that test, bro? Cause I'm missing work here because your company dropped the ball."

"Two days," he said somewhat defeated, and I just rolled my eyes and shrugged, fully expecting a letter to arrive by mail from the Academy announcing my nomination for best new actor of the year. Then I feel a warm trickle down my legs and realize I never closed the lid to the bottle and with each passing second was pissing myself more and more in front of the man. I would have to skip the encore, and got out of there as quickly as possible.

I enter my car, and the radio station I had left on was playing "Eye of the Tiger." I twist the dial until it snaps off and smoke that first cigarette in two whole breaths. By the time I turn the corner out of the plant you can hear my tires squealing and a maniac screaming, "Went the distance, now I'm not going to stop, Just a jit and his will to survive!"

That whole incident scared me straight for at least a while, so I stopped smoking weed, and my alcoholism ran in full, societally accepted, bore. What a stupid world we live in. I was still good for the occasional toot of crystalized molly from my Korean raver boys on a wild Friday night, and listen, I wasn't applying for sainthood, I just wanted to weld pipes together. But allow this story to be a lesson to you, my fellow scumbags: if given the opportunity, use the piss hot from the tap instead of some chemical mixture you pick up from a dildo shop.

Two days later, I was back on the job with a fire under my ass so hot to prove to these men who knew nothing about me that I wasn't a drug addict creep and could actually be an asset to the crew.

"So what drugs are you on, kid?" Gonzo asks me this knowing full well I somehow walked on water during this whole ordeal. I still trusted no one in this business and just hit him back with the appropriate political answer.

"What I find works best is to do a little bit of everything. That way when the panel lights up like a Christmas tree, the only logical conclusion is malfunction rather than complete human degeneracy." Gonzo nodded his head in agreement.

The Gonz Man was a swinger, and he would shamelessly tell anyone about it that would listen. He was somewhere in his fifties with a bridge earring and a handful of tattoos carefully placed around his body as if the layout came to him from a tri-fold brochure that fell out of the sleeve of that book *The Pick-Up Artist*.

"Kid, you into pee?" Flashbacks to my recent ordeal trigger a thousand-yard stare recognizable only in legless veterans and husbands exiting *CATS*.

"That's a negative, Gonz," I tell him.

"Tonight, I want you to stop at Home Depot and get yourself one of those blue tarps."

"I'm not..."

"You drape that over your bed and have your old lady piss on you, brother. It's going to change your life. That's a direct order, soldier."

I saluted the man and tried to put it out of my mind. *I have my own fetishes to contend with, thank you very much.* Later in the job he would encourage me to stay at his mountain home.

"Anytime you want. You go up there, I got a lake, we're close to the mountain. You ski? You and your girl, you don't pay me nothing."

"Thanks, man, I..."

"All I ask is"—*Yup, there it is*—"that you leave one *used*, has to be used, pair of your girl's panties on my pillow."

I thanked him sincerely as I knew by now the offer was not in jest and told him I would think about it. I should have taken him up on it and left a pair of my own. Leave that scent scrambling around his brain for a few days. Despite the madness, I felt this gravitational pull grow stronger as it flushed me closer towards the event horizon known only as: Steamfitter.

The job was pipeline, but it was simple enough. One pig launcher, one pig receiver, and between the two a metering skid with the pipe and valves and reliefs that connected it all together. We also erected a small flare tower where the reliefs, if activated, would empty into a two-inch underground stainless line that ran about a football field away to the tiny flare. With the knowledge I possess now, the job was sort of a lay-up, but the contractor we were working for at the time had never bid pipeline work before, and so ran it like it was any old industrial project, and forsook the necessary finesse, equipment, and schmoozing required of underground work under the 1104 welding code and to stroke the tender egos of *pipeliners*. Subsequently, it would be the most fucked up job I was ever on, but I learned a lot. Mostly, I learned how to work. Really. Fucking. Work.

Randy was a Napoleonic little *downhilling* rig welder, and if I hadn't become fast friends with about one of his only allies in the local, Steve Russo, he would have treated me like a stain too. At first, I was assigned as the man's helper, which means after he ran his root pass, it was my responsibility to grind any high spots or trapped slag per the welder's specification. Randy used a nine-inch grinder with a nine-inch wheel on it, and the weight and centrifugal force of the thing in motion was like wrestling a bull that could *seppuku* your innards out all over the dirt if you weren't strong enough to handle the kicks. As the man welded, it was my responsibility to work his remote in increments of up five or down five, which was a rough percentage of the total amperage the machine was set to on the back of his rig. Randy drove a black Dodge 3500 duelly, with blacked out CM truck bed in the back, and if memory serves me, he welded with a red face Lincoln 300 classic D, but I could be mistaken. As boring as it could be at times, my attention to Randy's commands was imperative as there are limited ways a *downhilled* puddle can be manipulated and maintained, and the only way to wrangle it and make it do what you want was to alter the amperage as you were welding. I frequently zoned out, and this drove these pipeliners insane, as it would drive me insane now as a downhiller myself some eight years later.

Regan was Randy's *brother-in-law* on the job. That's an industry term for the guy that welds the other side of the pipe with you on any pipe fourteen inches in diameter and above. He was the polar opposite of his helper, Gonzo, in personality, and they absolutely hated each other. Both of them spoke of their own genitalia frequently, however, and very likely had had a quite literal dick measuring contest on the job. Randy and Regan were convinced Gonz was a homosexual, based on that swinger lifestyle he could never stop talking about. Gonz would even admit to the screeched halt of the men, "Yeah, I'm BI-sexual. I buy sex all the time!" And it's that kind of tongue in cheek shit I would pull years later as I tucked my flowing locks under my weld cap, concealed a seamless bra under my gear, and chomped down estrogen pills in the morning. Hmm, who knows? Maybe he really was bisexual.

The first few weeks went pretty much like that. Sixty hours of grinding carbon steel pipe and twisting remote dials in a field along a lone stretch of highway. At least I wasn't sweating it out in a rubber suit back in the hydrofluoric acid unit I'd come from in the refinery. Supervision must have realized they were falling behind on the underground stainless lines and so transferred Luke Conti to the project, a premier stainless TIG welder whose reputation was known by almost everyone in the local. He would become my great friend and mentor, and at times serve almost like a father to me.

Conti was stoic and reserved and not nearly as visibly insane as the rest of the men I had met so far in this business. He was a savvy stock investor and blue-collar businessman, and because of his work ethic and initiative he owned a sizable fishing boat down the shore that most referred to as the Yacht. His hands were less like human digits and more like the rough padded paws of some creature spawned out of Zeus's infidelity. Best of all, he came up in the eighties and so could regale you with stories so real and raw they make what I will eventually tell you sound like the yapping of some small, inconsequential mutt.

"See back then, most ironworkers in the city were Native American..." he tells me as I adjust the alignment bolts on the Sumner Ultra Clamp straddling the two-inch stainless joint he is preparing to weld.

"Something to do with their religion, like the higher they went in elevation the closer they were to God."

"No shit?" I reply, which is the appropriate reply to nearly everything anyone could possibly say to you in this business.

"And they all smoked weed. There were no harnesses or safety bullshit in the eighties. You could wear a belt if you wanted to, and although it might save your life it would break your back if you actually fell from any heights. And so we're all up there inching along the I-beams like a damn sloth, while these Native American guys are stepping over you passing joints back and forth between them."

"Wow," I say. "What a time to be alive." I have concluded, after listening to countless stories from old veterans about their times during the eighties, that I would not have survived the decade and figure it was probably fate that birthed me in a time of more insanely stringent safety protocols.

"That was nothing. When we were building the Nuke"—he was referring to the nuclear power plant on the outskirts of our territory—"they had a trailer for everything. You wanted to gamble, you go to the card trailer. Drink and a couple toots? There was a trailer for that. They even had a whore trailer, dude. They had a weekly auction and if you won it, it was a day off with pay, a gun, and an hour in the whore trailer." Truly God's kingdom actualized on Earth, or at least that is likely what I thought at the time.

But more than just old war stories, Luke gave me something invaluable: a skill few possessed. They put us in an old C-box we converted into the stainless fabrication shop, because you can't have wind blowing away your argon purge when you're TIG welding stainless (or anything for that matter), and so we baked in that steel oven all summer long. Every chance I could, I stood over the man's shoulder and watched his welding technique. Conti put his roots in cold and utilized the dab and keyhole method, which is just one of a thousand ways to skin the proverbial cat, but it allowed the man to rest easy knowing that the internal sidewalls were properly breaking down because he could physically see it happen. Years later, I would evolve past the technique and use the southern-fried *back feed* method, which in my opinion is the superior method at least in terms of speed and fill, but I'd never let my *sensei* know the grasshopper might have surpassed him. I always liked life better as the student rather than the teacher, and never minded my time under the tutelage of Luke Conti.

The metal follows the heat, Chucky. I still hear Conti's words run through my mind every time I run a stainless root.

Baking in the oven completely nude would have been bad enough, but safety protocols from the contractor we were working for demanded we wear green welding jackets and pancake respirators so as to protect ourselves from the hexavalent chromium sprayed into our breathable air via dust and fume. The way it was explained to me is that stainless dust never rusts or disintegrates or gets expelled from the body like carbon steel will, and so after some years of confusion, the body starts attacking the microscopic particles as an unwanted intruder and lung cancer forms at the site of internal battle. So, we would bake alive neatly bundled, sucking breath through a rubber bladder that would collect our sweat and spit in pools of grime around our lips.

And all this under the watchful eye of safety *jit*, Dick Torres, who would lay in the brush in a ghillie suit and binoculars a quarter mile away making sure we were adhering to code even when we thought nobody was looking. Now, if you told me old Dicky had forty severed Vietnamese heads neatly arranged in a series of basement freezers for preservation until the eventual blood ritual, well, I'd buy that without even blinking. And don't take the Vietnamese thing with too much salt, it's just if Dick actually DID have forty severed heads in his basement, I feel like race or some other unifying prerequisite would need to be present in the case. At least that's my rough-cut psychological profile. Safety man by day, Vietnamese heads by night. Kind of a big sweety to me though. That being said, I did catch him measuring my skull once.

"Gentlemen. They're moving me to material man. This guy Garvin's coming in taking my spot as GF," Nash informed us in the trailer late one Friday afternoon well into the job.

Al Garvin's reputation preceded him. By the men's standards, he was either tolerated or hated and there was nothing in between. It would be my interpretation that those with half a head on their shoulders had to at least respect the knowledge base that the man possessed. Seemed those who struggled with mechanical concepts or failed in ability of clairvoyance to read both his mind and mood hated him, but then again Garvin couldn't stand nitwits and his bedside manner was less than par in an industry where par was measured by how well you could "shut the fuck up" and "shrug it off." He had a plethora of nicknames, and as I traveled with him over the years, it seemed the well of future names would never run dry. I was particularly fond of Lobsterman and Purple Face, as he was a lifelong alcoholic and years of gin and cigarettes left his nose disfigured and his face the color of a plum especially when he was angry, which was most of the time. He smoked Parliament cigarettes like they were the breath of God, and so had a permanently yellow stain dyed into his gray mustache and maybe even the skin below. There was also a pretty terrible rumor floating around about Garvin that I'll never reprint or speak of for that matter because I don't know for sure, but all I have to say about that is, either it's true, and that's really bad, or it's not, and that might even be worse. And you can read into that whatever you like.

Truthfully, they brought Garvin in as the closer. GQ had run that job absolutely into the ground because he was more concerned with sneaking off and spending time at home, which was only a few miles away, or lying in the brush as a bushman hunter sniping deer with a .22 caliber rifle in an active tank farm and pipeline facility. GQ was a conspiratorial, far right nutjob, and I used to joke the inside of his hardhat was lined in tinfoil. He hilariously bolted together every spool piece prefabbed for the job a quarter mile away in an open field in a dangerous rats nest amalgamation of pipe and bolts that reached maybe twenty feet vertical at points in preparation for an eventual hydrostatic pressure test. Proper technique would be to pressure test everything once properly installed and in its final location and bypass damage to the valves by constructing "valve replacement spools." Then, after the hydro test was *bought off*, drop the spools, install the valves, and be done with it, instead of lugging a hundred-some thousand pounds of steel back and forth a quarter mile through a field that would turn to complete mud and slop at the first sign of humidity. I use the word *hilarious* only to drive a small self-tapping screw into the man's ego, but I was the stupid bastard that had to bolt all those pieces together and the work was back-breaking because the novice, because that's what he was and likely still is, ordered twelve by twelve pieces of dunnage that had to weigh easily over a hundred pounds, and it was the only material we had to rest and erect the pipe upon. Mostly though, GQ was a delusional hypocrite, my greatest insult next to *politician*, and on that single hand used to cup water from the runoff of a small-time ball-washing operation, GQ was the middle finger.

"GQ, we have a problem..." His boots were crossed over one another resting on his desk and he lifted his eyes from his phone.

"Well, Luke and I were going over the weld maps with the inspector and it looks like some of this pipe was double fabbed." By some of the pipe, I mean like fifty additional unnecessary welds. He looked like he was going to puke. The job was already turning on him, not to mention he was quick enemies with Garvin, who I guess technically held his life in his hands.

"How could you do that?!" Immediately, like a true spanked poodle, he deflected.

"Uh, well, now, hold on a second....See, I dated every drawing you gave me, and not for nothing, but Luke and I never received a rundown of this job. We've been in that hotbox for the last three months fabricating whatever drawing you gave us." He looked shook. The weasel in his mind ran faster on the wheel. It would come back to me that he told Garvin it was all my fault. Garvin wasn't that stupid and was disgusted by the act, as anyone should be.

Fortunately, because I came from the world of the white collar, I documented the date of every weld made as well as the issuance from GQ on the date I received the drawing. I was never given a run down or overview of the entirety of what we were constructing, but only the piecemeal prints of the fabricable spools we could make in a shop setting before eventual field welds. Basically, I had all the evidence to indicate not only was GQ lying, but he was also committing one of the most despicable acts in this business: throwing an apprentice under the bus, be it his fault or not. He would do this again years later to a classmate of mine, and yet still, to this day he is in a supervisory position, his head even bigger than when we first met. Hey, GQ, if you're reading this, if I ever kissed your ass it will be the heaviest burden I take with me to the grave. Also, are you hiring?

The end of this project was likely the hardest I ever worked in my life. Fourteen-hour day minimums going upwards of twenty-two-hour days and back in at seven in the morning, seven days a week for a heavy month of hell. The few hours I slept, I would ask questions about the job in my sleep, and my girlfriend just stared at me in some mixture of concern and horror. I would be so tired on those three a.m. rides home, I would drive with all the windows down in the winter with the radio blasting and just yelling as loud as I could to keep myself conscious. Sometimes even that didn't work, and it was the rumble strips that kept me awake and got me home.

Then, like the passing of some terrible storm, it was over. Most of the men were laid off or transferred, and it was me and Garvin who remained to polish off the punch list items the client had wanted completed before startup. We were back on a lazy eight hours, and one day around noon, Garvin asked me what I wanted to do.

"Strip club," I said jokingly.

He exhaled smoke through his nose. "Ok."

That would be the start of Garvin's and my legitimate friendship. Afternoons at an old man go-go joint in the city that actually made a pretty good roast pork sandwich. He would download the problems of management in my head and question my intention of being a welder, rather than aiming straight for upper management.

"You can train any monkey to weld, kid." Spoken like a guy who never welded.

"It's about respect. I couldn't respect someone who orders you to do the task but can't do it themselves, so why should I expect anything different if I bypass the hard way?" I told him.

"Fuck respect, make the money." That's where we differed. I never gave a fuck about the money. Truth is, I couldn't do any other type of work now. The fitters had already ruined me. How could I look myself in the mirror, cashing checks from writing emails rather than running a slick root and cap that stops both amateur and veteran alike and has them question "Who welded that?"

Garvin could drink with the best of them. He diagnosed my perceived sobriety as the result of a hollow leg. Truth is, I just wasn't on drugs, and there were very few people at that time who could drink more than me if I was just using alcohol. One particular Thursday afternoon would stand out amongst the choppy history of my alcoholic debauchery as psychologically telling, be you Freudian analyst or drooling imbecile.

We had started at two in the afternoon at the Handlebar in the city, which was a safe haven for union tradesmen to drink and fight and socialize without the discriminatory stares of the more polished mass of society. Where a topless stripperette served Pabst Blue Ribbon specials in her panties and cowgirl hat beneath the glow of two ancient box TV sets that transmitted ball games between static and interference. After Garvin departed at about six, sufficiently sloshed, I hung around and switched to whiskey, and handed the keys over to this other creature who was motivated by more reptilian desires. I would close my eyes and when they opened again, I was at the bar next door speaking to some woman convinced I was Donnie's brother. I certainly was not.

"Yeah, I'm Donnie's brother," I tell her.

"I knew it! I'm going to text him right now!"

"Yeah, go ahead. Tell him his brother says he's a big bag of shit." And she did it, and it wasn't even funny by now that I had gotten so good at this fake identity shit. If I had wanted to, I could have landed her, but I didn't. What was it I wanted?

Then, a trans girl walked into the bar with a group of friends I would have categorized as *dweebus* at that time in my life, and I clocked her near immediately like all closeted trans or trans-infatuated individuals can do regardless of how well the person passes. Thinking back, it is sort of funny from the perspective of that girl who so wanted to get into my pants, as I drifted past her mid-sentence to approach this trans woman. Certainly must have been a blow to her self-esteem. With any luck she gave up the bar scene entirely, donned the black habit, and spent the rest of her years pacing around a convent contemplating the animal desires of the twisted and damned. I made a fool of myself in front of this transwoman. If I spoke it was in garbled nonsense words wrapped in the spittle and moisture of hot, odorous breath that came out too close to her face. I can't remember what I said to the poor girl. I'm sure I lacked the finesse to allude to her transness as impulse told me to do, but it probably came out more like, "I know what you are?" And so, one of her scrawny friends put his hand on my shoulder and told me it was time to go. And so I just left. And I heard my voice in the room and in my head.

I know what you are.

Now all of this was remembered in hindsight and pieced together over the following days and weeks because by now I was riding the line of nearly completely blacked out. Some voice in my head said, "Just do it." And so, I did. I paid my tab and started making my way to my vehicle. What was it I was doing?

I had some rough intention of heading to the city's gay neighborhood and lied to myself that I just wanted to see a trans person in the flesh. That it could be done. That one could transition and have the courage to walk around outside in public like a regular fucking human. But that was a bullshit lie my unconscious mind told my walking form, and a more accurate depiction of reality was I was nothing more than the lurking goblin in the shadows.

I blink again and I'm behind the wheel and immediately realize I'm WAY too inebriated to be driving. I pull over right then and there. Where I parked, I had no recollection. Once on the sidewalk I flagged a taxi, and when the driver asked me where I wanted to go, I told him, "You know."

"What?" he said, and my head was resting against the rear passenger windshield, too drunk to stay erect.

"You know where. You know where I want to go. Take me to the spot." Why do I feel this strange sensation of déjà vu?

"Yeah, I know where you want to go."

He drove for a few minutes and parked at the start of a lone dark alley. Then he said, "You walk down there halfway and it's on your left." I grunted and handed him a fistful of bills. It must have been sufficient payment because he wasn't screaming or beating me to death in the street. Then I staggered off, not really knowing exactly where he had taken me.

I was ushered into a red lit room of Asian women in lingerie. None of them looked transgender to my eyes, which bulged like two abscessed warbles ready to burst with fresh parasitic larva.

"Right this way." She had me by the forearm, but I broke her grasp.

"I need to use the restroom."

"Over there." She pointed, visibly irked by my drunkenness.

Once inside, I let crawl out of me some heinous wretchedness

I would be embarrassed to expel in my own domicile, isolated in the far reaches of the Antarctic, let alone an underground Asian washy-wash. My phone rings. It's Michelle. And God. With the sound and vibration of its ringing I'm whisked through a wormhole of poor decision making back into thinking reality. Where the fuck was I?

"Hey, babe."

"Chuck, you're drunk. Where are you?" The voice of a broken heart.

"Had to pull over and take a shit, babe. Heading home now."

"You can't drive!"

"It's okay, I took a taxi." I try to explain but it doesn't sound right even to me as it comes out of my mouth.

"What are you talking about? You worked today."

"That's right. Either way, I'll be home soon." There's banging at the door and untranslatable sounds of aggravated Asian women. I end the call and open the bathroom door to a mama-san with a cane that could either club your lights out or be used to keep herself standing upright depending on what was required at that moment.

I walked right past her for the main door.

"No, you can't leave!" she hollered. But I just ignored her, broke through the door, and sprinted up the street and back into the fray of the normal public. And that would be the weirdest shit I ever took in my life.

How did I get here? I thought. I took a cab back to the Handlebar, figuring I never would have been stupid enough to get behind the wheel. Once there, I see that my car isn't parked where I originally left it over eight hours ago and jump to the conclusion that it must have been stolen by some deranged lunatic, which wasn't entirely inaccurate. I kick in the door to the Handlebar.

"Who stole my fucking car!" The bouncer raised one quick, meaty paw up to my throat and pushed me back towards the door. I nearly fell on my ass.

"No one. You're having a bad night, aren't you?" he asked, but I didn't answer.

I went back outside to the scene of the crime and concluded it must have gotten towed. Yeah, that was it. The rear bumper was four inches over a no parking line and the parking author-ity in this city is worse than Hitler's own private SS. I figured I'll just have to get it in the morning before work, and call my third cab of the evening.

Once back in my neighborhood, I stop at an ATM and with-draw one hundred dollars cash. I fumble the money and it falls from my fingers and when I look for it on the ground it has com-pletely disappeared. One hundred dollars was a lot to lose at that time in my life, especially so absolutely stupidly, and I think I cried in the street.

Back at the apartment, Michelle said nothing to me, and I slept like death for a few hours until memory and hangover shot through my skull like two defibrillator pads plugged directly into my temples. I had a panic attack on the carpet, and I cried that I didn't want to drink anymore.

There was a string tied to my finger and it told me my car had been towed, but that didn't feel right. And so, after calling the impound lot at six and having them run my license to no avail, I started to remember a different series of events from that which my final conclusion prior to unconsciousness had indicated. I borrowed Michelle's car and headed in the vague direction of the neighborhood of my initial intention.

The city was still mostly asleep at this hour, and I drove around block by block with the windows down and my arm and car keys hanging out, pressing the alarm button so I could find my ve-hicle by nothing other than sonar. I had let Garvin know I was going to be a little late. We had a hell of a day in front of us and I could not miss work. I was just about to end my search when I heard it. Beep beep.

"What the fuck was that!" And again, beep beep.

"Holy shit!" I turned the corner and there she was, double parked in front of a municipal building with blood red no park-ing signs littering the sidewalk and a tow truck lowering the bed to haul my vehicle out of there. The men preparing to tow my car stood around in complete confusion as to why it was beep-ing. Then I pulled up next to them and said, "I'll move that car right now; don't tow it!"

"What are you going to do with the one you're driving?"

"Uh…" There was a lot across the street. "I'll leave it over there. Give me one minute!"

"You got one minute!" They started raising the bed on their tow truck.

Once back in old trusty, I called Garvin and let him know I'd be there by eight, that my car had gotten towed, and I just got it out. I was certainly still drunk.

On the job, he chuckled at my physical and emotional pain and probed the inconsistencies of my story, but once identifying the telltale squirming of a man grasping at straws, relented in his questioning, likely concluding something entirely different happened than what I regaled him with. And why wouldn't he at least show me that mercy, as he was certainly a man with his own vast closet full of skeletons.

I wouldn't drink or do drugs for eight months after this incident, and instead dedicated myself to my work, growing a reputation as a fine young fitter who spent his off hours practicing welding, and doing my best to leave not a minute of the day for thought or reflection.

CHAPTER 4

HATE

No. We're not writing about hate. Not this morning, not after the Lord blessed me with a few hours of steady sleep. But in that pregnant emptiness of night, that catalytic churning of the itchy mind, a tornado against blue skies rages far out on the cerebral prairies, and what's worse, there's nothing of value to raze except the parts of the brain that rest cakey and low like the hard pan of the high plains. A tempest too restless to realize the fronts had long since married and the storm had left you alone to fizzle out in the West.

I thought a lot about buckshot in the night, and how I could wield it against my enemies and against myself. And so, I pitched my legs over the side of the bed, and I felt hot and dry, and plugged the tender pulse of my temples with open palms if for no other reason than to keep my brain from expanding beyond the limits of my skull.

A crackle of fireworks froths in sparkly decrescendo from the parking lot beyond my property, and I think it's only in the silence of its erratic percussion that my son stirs in his crib and lets out one very forceful and deliberate, "Muuum!" My wife hinges upright like the reborn dead and stares ahead with the half-eyed, semi-gloss fatigue of the seemingly eternal sleeplessness that is newborn motherhood. She cradles my son, and the warmth of his mother's arms is enough recipe to recreate the ever-elusive elixir that is true rest. And then her nails tickle up my spine and my nerves take in this exotic, electric binary that cuts white light signals through this bitter vigil, and those shadowy parts seem significantly smaller during those flashbulb flickers of light from out the mind's sky.

"What's wrong?" She says this louder than she normally would despite the sleeping boy.

"I think I want to shoot my parents with a shotgun." And then I whine on about not sleeping, and that I'm dry, and that I can't write at night.

And so then I said, "I guess I'll just read."

And then I read Bukowski for a little bit, and then some Cormac, and then Dumas. Somewhere into Tesla I fall asleep. And sleep solid for the first time in eight days.

Fifteen-minute Coffee

CHAPTER 5

SEX

You must understand, this book took me three years to write. This next part I wrote during the pandemic, just before I started medical transition. At the time, it was the truest thing to come out of me, at a period in my life where fiction and reality had collided in pyrotechnic shimmer, when anything reached for dissolved right there at the touch, leaving no more evidence of its existence than a small epidermal burn. To put it in plain speak...it can feel very crazy.

My opinions and reasons regarding personal transition have devolved greatly since this first small truth came out of me. I think that's how truth works. It comes first in heavy vernacular, too complicated to contain in one mental snapshot: you piece it together like a detective's evidence board with all the multicolored strings and pins and photographs of a bigger picture you can't quite render. Then one day, staring ahead at this psychedelic birds' nest growing out of your wall and sucking into it every stupid thought of your whole damn life, you see it. Smack dab in the middle of it all. It was Keyser Söze the whole damn time. But I can't give you that yet. You've got to walk with me through the fire first, and see in the end how simple it was all along.

By this point, I accept myself. But this damn virus keeps postponing the date for these drugs they tell me will set me right. I move onward through time and space and decision towards that date where the balance on the scale of emotion tips more to anticipation than fear, and my anxiety wells only from a place of further delayed acquisition of what my mind tells me are my body's proper chemicals.

There's this word I'm going to use only once in this book: *dysphoria.* And I'm only going to use it once because no one really knows what it means, even those who are crippled by it. You can probably best grasp footage of the word by visions of the anti-Christ, whatever that is in your mind, be it goat-headed men or cloven-footed pigs of political disposition, or a wretched green storm ushered in by apocalyptic horsemen, or death, or worst of all, loneliness. My point is, it is a sort of very precise vague concept, a toxic slurry in the waterways of your life, and from it spawn creatures of the worst types of thought. Ones that only speak in self-hate. They use words like Freak and Monster. Pervert. Fetish. Creep. Loser. And Kill Yourself. The vilest of these visions are warped mirror reflections of yourself and they pal around you, crummy at first, and then once their tendrils fish under your flesh and cinch into your ribcage and your spine they grow bulbous with puss, and sore and red and stinking, and they piss out little pockets of air and ooze and the whispered release of gas sounds just like, "Kill Yourself." And you'll shift your weight and free some other trapped pocket, and maybe you're just at work or you're trying to sleep, and it'll whisper, "Kill Yourself." Sometimes you might even thumb shells into the shotgun of life when these magicians conduct cacophonies with all the other vile ooze-spawn of your mind, and you're just sort of on auto-pilot if for no other reason than one final loud crack and then sweet blank frequency.

I'd ask you then to stay your hand. For I have been where you've been, or where you may go. And listen hard through those hapless hisses because there is a voice that never dies; it is your voice, it is the kernel of your core, and it is incorruptible. Some call that God. But you can believe in it or deny it in whatever way feels right for you. Just, next time, when you're thumbing shells into the shotgun of life, listen through that griping mess. The funny part is you might not hear it. You might not hear that voice I speak of. I know I didn't. But I looked for it. I stopped and I listened...

You know, the less I saw God in the world, the more I wanted to be like Him, and prove to the nonbelievers that She really does exist. I think you have to have that thought, or something like it, to hear the voice again. And then you might just be invincible. Killed only by one thing: the period mark of life. But it won't be you who spears your own tendon. That much I'm sure of.

Now that all that hopefulness is out of the way, I've been feeling bad. It seems like whatever that word means amplified in its effect once I fully accepted my identity. And so now, I feel brutish, like an ogre, and I suffer from insomnia in ways I never have before. My biggest fear is the job, and the future, and money. Like anyone. We are seeds cast in rocky soil. Succulents of the prickliest variety. Creeping molds grown in the shit and the dark. But I don't want to live here anymore. I want to burn in the light of the day. Like anyone, I guess.

But then she kisses me in the night. And I feel like a mental case, and she kisses me again. And I say the kids are sleeping and she says, "Shhhh." After it all I hold her, and feel radiating between us a true divine healing, and I sleep unstirred all the way into the morning.

CHAPTER 6

HELL'D BACK

Let's go back, shall we? Just for a brief reprieve. What sort of up-bringing and life events contribute to a psychology that would so readily throw away their hyper-masculine reputation for one of modest femininity, which in my industry is akin to licking the open sores of syphilitic lepers. Now, just over two years into hormonal transition yet still closeted professionally, I see a tidal break forming in the sea of men (mostly men) of my union hall, where if I present much more of my true self, I'll be able to push the waters back entirely before they come to their senses and maybe crush me to death.

But I digress. I would be lying to you if I said I hadn't looked at this from every possible angle: positive, negative, scientifically backed or conspiratorial. I've read scholarly journals on the subject matter of transgenderism and its effects on life, limb, and the rearing of young children. I've approached the subject from a psychoanalytic, cognitive, Jungian, Christian, and Buddhist philosophical perspective and drawn conclusions of granite in the morning that would shatter like glass by the night. But I'm rambling. For this brief reprieve, I'm just going to show you what it was like growing up and let you draw your own conclusions if I'm sane or shattered.

CHAPTER 7

THIRTEEN

Her name was Crystal, but maybe it was with a "K", and I was mean as hell to the poor girl. She was thirteen when I knew her, or maybe twelve, cursed with large breasts and small shirts, and I was just a year her senior. She was an obnoxious little thing, but she liked me, so much so I could see it in her eyes, and I liked anyone who could like me.

During our private times on the bus after the bullies left, I could be nice to her. And the soft parts of our spirits could spill out past our Walmart wardrobes, and kind innocence could flourish for two bus stops before our fictitious contest renewed arms in the recognition of tomorrow's school day.

"Yeah, I'll take you to the movies." It was her stop, but she stayed seated.

"Really?" And that word hung there in space for all eternity with that hopeful uncertainty that maybe our false war could really be over.

"Yeah," I said, and I meant it. My heart flapping in my chest as the undertow of social commitment drew me closer to the girl and wonderful curls of naive pleasure crashed against my rock-face ribcage and tides of rushing blood flow broke back only at the slender tips of my fingers and toes.

And she got up and she smiled and didn't say anything and pressed her toes deep into the soil when she stepped down from the bus and skipped all the way back to her trailer.

The following afternoon the bullies sneered. They outnumbered me with their laughter and socially I was weak.

"Ew, you like Crystal?" The truth is a heavy beam of light that tackles the weak and the strong ride like a wave.

"Who said that?" I look back at the girl sitting in a seat in the middle of the bus, and her eyes dart downward with frightened instinct but only momentarily, and tepid they rose back to meet mine as though maybe there was truth in yesterday's words.

I look back at the fat hick, his nose upturned like a hog's, and he would squeal when his pudgy logic could grab hold of some weakness in the other and pull it down in the mud with him. Then he says that Crystal said it. That I was going to take her to the movies. That she was gross and I by rumored allegiance. And I felt that crippling loneliness from my earlier childhood, and I had long since made resolve to never experience that again.

"Yeah, I said that." And their eyes widen in my admission of guilt, salivating over my tender scraps. The moist, fat-ribboned flanks of myself truffled out below the ribs and beyond the tasteless tendons.

"But I wasn't going to go…" *Yes, I was.*

"I just said that, and I, I was going to leave her hanging…" *What am I saying?*

"Yeah, I don't like Crystal. Who could like Crystal? She's a pig."

"You're evil, Keiran." They slapped my back and knuckled my sides and felt that hardened casing that was my outside flesh, and reaffirmed that I was one of them. And so I didn't have to be alone. And I was akin to hogs.

That little girl cried her eyes out the whole way home. And I can't remember exactly, but I don't think she rode the bus anymore after that. It was close to the end of the school year anyway, and that summer I moved away. Likely, coming from where we came from, next to her father, I was the first mean bastard in a long life of mean bastards for that girl.

Sometimes, once I got to Philly, alone in that first apartment before the moving madness started, I would think about the big breasted girl with small shirts, and spend the next seventeen years of my life fantasizing how it must feel to be so beautifully cursed.

CHAPTER 8

SPARKY

Sparky was a good dog. I got him in the mountain view house. Must have been fourth grade, where the market of my school day popularity saw a two-year downtrend ending ultimately in my removal from that acrid grade school, where even the holy sisters burned in colors of vibrant salt as the chemical reaction of my childhood burned away the lacquer of my humble shell and revealed something significantly more rebellious.

My dad built him a chicken coop in the basement out of scrap two-bys and chicken wire because he didn't like dogs and he didn't want him upstairs where the carpets rippled pristine right up to the ice cream walls. And so, in the early days of Sparky, I sat in the coop with him. Eventually I would break my parents down and get that dog upstairs and even into my bed. I liked that my dog liked sleeping in the room with me.

I'm not going to lie and claim I was some great dog whisperer. Not at that age, at least. I was a child. And like a child, I both loved and neglected that dog in polarized turbulence swung one way or the other by fluctuations in attention span or ranked in priority by the day's expected fun or boredom or pain. But, not unlike my relationship with God, I would come crawling back. Mostly in my desperate times, when there was nothing else to turn to, there was this hazel-eyed dog that studied the world damn-near-human and even frightened false souls with his omnipotent glare.

Uncle Rust, who wasn't an uncle but rather one of those friends so close to the family he was honored with the brotherly title, was a Kenzo cop on the force with my father. Rust played the lottery every single night and when he lost he would call his mother and say, "Shittin' numbers!" He was also quick to launch into tirades about African Americans, although he never spoke of them in terms that remotely endearing. Well, at some point, maybe before I was born or maybe in my early years, Rust hit that lottery for five million dollars and moved to the Poconos not far from where we lived. He set the bar of the term "eccentric" so high that all those formerly defined by the word should just be forever rounded down into the greater bulk of chess aficionados and investment bankers and all those categorized by a life lived decidedly lesser than a Kensington man with a little money. At least he spent his money on the fun things in life, and although by now he's probably dead or doesn't have two nickels to rub together, he was my first taste outside of the family of the Other. Of a road less traveled. Less structured. A real true wild man caged by neither the city nor the forests. And he'd let me drive his golf cart like it was a damn dune buggy.

Uncle Rust didn't drink as I recall. But one time, he was drunk. Pretty piss drunk. And Sparky was with us at his house for some reason, which means it wasn't during the time when we lived with Rust, which is another story and a different dog entirely. Rust would always comment on that dog's hazel eyes. The man had no faith, and he especially hated nuns. But he could almost talk about things that sounded like reincarnation when he talked about that dog and his eyes. And on that piss drunk day, where my parents were I can't remember, he screamed at my dog and said in one loud burst, "Stop looking at me!" And he stormed upstairs, and he slammed his door, and I picked up Sparky, who seemed totally unaffected by the bizarre outburst.

Sparky was used to outbursts by that point, I'm sure. Back before Sparky, when it was just me, and Mom, and Dad, Mom would curl me up into her bed after the fight and whisper in my ear, "If you turn out like your father, I'll kill you." And then we could cry together, a five-year-old and his mother, and I would say, "I won't, Mama. I won't."

Years later, after the *Realization*, I would walk out into the field with Sparky and sit up on the sand mound with him where he liked to shit. We'd find some untouched piece of grass, and I would hold him there even though he didn't like to be held that long, and like a young fool I'd look back at the house and feel my rage resound like a gong with every smashed dish and every fruitless shriek. And the sage mutt in his sapience looked the other way at a mountain range like the bursting fist of God, blue and green and low-tone browns. A place of perfect peace. And there in the center of it all, a lake punctuated by scratch-mark water vessels that would light up the night with little pen-light period marks of the third-shift fishermen trolling for bass or bluegill, or maybe cat or black crappie. It's only in my memory that I imagine the dog's wisdom. But back then. There on the shit hill. I think the only thing running through my mind was the under-formed vocalizations of parental hate. I don't like to use that word now, and even then, I would never dare utter it aloud and give it life. But knowing me then and what was to come, yeah, I think pretty objectively that must have been hate, if even just in its most innocent form.

Sparky broke his leash one day when I was walking him because the hillbillies with money at the bottom of the hill revved their dirt bikes too close to the dog and spooked him, and Spark just kept running in a straight line through the woods and over the hills and beyond the horizon where I couldn't track him anymore.

After I abandoned my personal search for Spark, we all piled into the car and scoured the woods and the backroads for the dog late into the night, screaming his name and "Snausages!" out the window because he was addicted to the treats and just saying the word could shatter his most stubborn verdicts. Even after I went to bed, our search having proved fruitless, my dad went out with his million-lumen flashlight and called to the dog that he didn't like on the couch, and even said "Snausages," although maybe not too loud.

In the morning, it was Mom and me, and we prayed one of those little hopeless prayers, some small prayer of duty to the Lord to show Him we were still aligned despite having lost this thing of such immense value. The prayer ended, and the Lord answered with one lone, exhausted scratch at the back door. Sparky had survived his dark night of the soul, and I filed the whole thing away under the evidence of magic maybe existing in this otherwise mundane world.

--- - --- - --- - --- - --- - --- - --- - --- - --- - --- - --- - --- - --- - --- - --- - --- - ---

Jay had a shit life. Although I never saw his father drink, he possessed all of the characteristics of a mean drunk, be he dry or otherwise. But the old man seemed downright altruistic against the backdrop of his grandmother, in both appearance and tone. Jay's grandmother was a mean old bitch who would put that twig boy down every chance she could, but Jay was too country good, and although he hated the woman, cause you could see it in his blue-fire eyes, he took every swat, day after day, right there on the chin and volleyed nothing back except, "Okay, Gram."

Jay was the start of new friendships in the Poconos. Up until then it was a few neighborhood kids, but most had moved away, and the one who had remained was a few years my senior and just over that tipping point where my friendship was a social impediment. But Jay and I could have fun in different ways. We liked to fish and explore the woods. And where Jay lived at the bottom of the hill, he had better woods. Less carved out. More rugged. Unattainable sections barricaded by thorny thickets that we had to chop through with makeshift machetes. And when we finally reached the far side of the woods, we would be bleeding and ivy soaked and our fresh cuts would sting with the poisons of the deep woods, and I think by the end of it all we both felt damn alive.

Jay had a dumb horse, and two dumb dogs, and some chickens that we would take crack shots at with a pellet rifle, judging our accuracy by the *ba-cawks* that would ring out like *bullseye*, and then we would snicker those mean, restless snickers known best to hill folks with good broken toys and the time and space to use them. Jay's dad whooped both our asses when he caught us firing at the birds, not because he didn't share in our same vicious humor because I think he did, but because the birds wouldn't lay eggs if you kept scaring them like that. And those eggs were a staple in that household.

By eighth grade, it was my reign as ruler of the mountain. Old kids moved away or got sucked into their rooms by developing computer tech, and young kids moved to the valley. So it was me and Jay and a handful of young 'uns, and we rode bicycles held together with scrap we salvaged at a yard a few miles away. And like rogue bandoleros or child Warlocks, we took all roads leading down, and in that brief descent, our shorts whipped up into our groins, we hooted like goblins or maybe charioteers. If only we could have just shut up for a second, we might have made out that pure, stark wind that cuts ripples in the mountain face and pokes clean ecstasy through your ears and into your mind where it stays for all the days of the rest of your life.

--- - --- - --- - --- - --- - --- - --- - --- - --- - --- - --- - --- - --- - --- - --- - --- - --- - ---

"Holy Ghost." They said that to me, and I must have looked back like I was hearing a punchline I didn't quite comprehend.

"It's an all-boys school." Like that was supposed to make it better.

If the Poconos was one thing to all of us seventh and eighth graders who lived there at that time, it was gay. Anything and everything that was bad or different was "gay," or maybe "quer." Not "queer" with two "e's," but "quer" because to elongate the "e" might have been a little too gay. Being gay was the worst thing someone could be there and then, and I honestly think Hitler affiliates were outlined in more sympathetic colors than the weak hues that all things gay were painted in. Needless to say, an all-boys school sounded very gay to me at that age and that time.

The conversation likely didn't go like this, but the flow of events surely did:

"It's a college prep school. The tuition is expensive, and Mommy and Daddy want the best for you. Here's a book. Study it. The test is in a few weeks. You're going. We're moving to Philly. Say goodbye to your friends." And that was eighth grade, in a nutshell.

Now I was in the honors class in eighth grade in that hillbilly public school. And that would start the opposite sex's fascination with me up until this very day, maybe. And I'm not going to lie, I loved it. But I remember one instance that bubbles up still at times during self-talks in the shower or mirror arguments. Mrs. Englert, or something gross like that. Some squirted out last name that could only be pronounced correctly if you squeezed the syllables out like the last crush of a tube of toothpaste. Mrs. Englert was a math teacher, and she didn't like me, but her daughter did. At this point it's sort of the pot calling the kettle black, but Mrs. Englert was an ugly woman inside and out, and I remember her most by her distinctly black mustache that she refused to wax or shave or what have you. And one day I'm talking in class, and her daughter says to me, "Wow, Chuck, your eyes are so black."

And without missing a beat, Mrs. Englert says, "What are those boys going to think about those black eyes next year?" The class erupted. At least she had comedic timing, I'll give her that.

When she turned her back, I gave her two middle fingers, and the class gasped if for no other reason than to draw attention to my irreverence and watch a punishment be doled out on someone that was already dead to them. I'd like to say she looked back at me like she'd messed up, but she didn't. I'd like to say I had some great comeback for her. I've certainly thought of a million of them over the years, but I didn't. She turned around and didn't say anything about the middle fingers, and smiled this little ignorant smile like she'd got to me. And she really did.

--- - --- - --- - --- - --- - --- - --- - --- - --- - --- - --- - --- - --- - --- - --- - --- - ---

"It's too expensive," Mom said, and with it she said she was sorry and still, to this day, I believe she was.

"What do you mean?" I can't remember if I was pissed or sad or scared.

"We can't find a place that takes dogs that isn't in a bad area. It's just too expensive; we can't afford it." That's both true and complete bull looking back now.

I could go into details about how the house they were selling was a geographic goldmine, despite the cheap price they sold it for. My dad was always afraid of "scaring the buyer off," and my brothers and I would just scratch our heads as missed opportunity after missed opportunity slipped through the fingers of our family's finances. Ultimately, that's a testament to my father's immense fairness. He possessed nothing of greed in his soul, and so couldn't take advantage of people, even if the advantage was warranted.

I could argue how keeping this familiar, loved thing, my dog, was of significantly more psychological value than living a couple of blocks into a "bad" neighborhood. Later on, we would move into a bad neighborhood to turn a profit on a flip property, so in the retrospective scheme of it all it was a lie. But at the time I bought it, and I tried to be strong, and they gave my dog away to a priest, and I came to learn what depression was for the first time in my life.

My mom bought me a computer after that, because we never had one of any worth, except a nearly inoperable IBM from my older brother's mortgage company. And a hamster. Prior to the new machine, I was writing my school papers on an old Brother word processor, which I actually liked and might even go back to at some point in my future. In fact, it was typewriters and word processors that started my affinity for the written word. I was writing stories even then, clacked out in blinking orange text and saved to a floppy disk called "Chuck's stuff," and I stored my private thoughts in a shoebox under my bed.

I think they were heartbroken, my parents, watching me play with that stupid rodent. I'd sing it songs and show my friends, and they'd cock their eyebrows that I had accepted the trade of a great dog for a stupid rat.

I think it was the spring before Holy Ghost. Before high school. And I think it was the day the computer got delivered to the house. I was excited. I could play games on it. The same games the kid next door played, and maybe we could play together. At least we'd have something to talk about. And when I ran downstairs to see the computer, Sparky was there, and I have never cried so hard in my entire life.

It took the dog a little while to warm back up to me. The story was, he had a hell of a time adjusting to life with the priest. He was a dog that roamed mostly off leash, and the priest lived in a convent or wherever the hell priests live, and I guess it took the man some time to train the dog to poop in a four-foot by four-foot square of grass rather than the fields of Elysium that Sparky was used to.

Mostly what I felt from Spark when he came back was a sense of uncertainty, that the memory of the dog isn't as shallow as man claims, and although maybe he couldn't piece together what exactly had happened, I guess I felt that Sparky was trying to grasp some concept of betrayal, although maybe he couldn't organize it into a logic.

What happens next would be a theme that would pervade well into the end of my childhood and stab on through my early adulthood, reeking and oozing and festering all the while until ultimately the wound it cratered would die off entirely and with it a large part of my empathy. That theme would be grandiose gestures of penance (often in the form of dogs) only to be scooped out like a wart and uprooted (often with the excuse of a new property). And all the while I was reminded how good I had it. How much better I had it than my brothers before me. How much better I had it than my own parents' childhoods. How grateful I should be. I was reminded of many things. All of them out of my control, be them good or ill. Truth is, I would have traded unblemished walls and pristine views of glorious mountain ranges and fighting and control and manipulation for the dogshit-laden basement and general clutter and laughter that my best friend Kenny's family offered.

They couldn't find another apartment. My mom had to start work as a nurse in the city. My dad had to stay behind and sell the mountain-view house, something that I know broke his heart in more ways than one. He had worked his absolute nuts to the bone to carve out his small slice of paradise. The shame of it is that the man is just about a genius, and yet it seemed like financial wellbeing would always be this fight rather than some leisure cruise. But I believe still, to this day, the move really was about getting me to a good school; it's just that something rotted along the way.

And so, we had to get rid of Sparky, again. And I think about Jay then. And his shit life, and his shit dogs, and his shit horse. His shit grandmother. His dad wasn't shit, he was just a dry drunk I think, but I don't know for sure. But of all the poor bastards who deserved that great dog, it was Jay. And he was good to that dog, I know it because I would check in on him from time to time, and years later Jay tracked me down and told me Sparky had died, and it didn't hurt quite as bad because by then we had Sparkied two more dogs. And that was that, as they say.

On my last day in the Poconos, we drove down the mountain view road, down below where Jay's house nestled up in the woods beyond a driveway of fractured pavement and modified stone of blue and gray and white, and I waved at the little cabin that housed my dog now and cried hard, heavy tears in the red, two-door Suburu that had stuffed in it every excess item of our country existence. Somewhere passed Allentown I stopped crying, and spent the rest of the day moving my parents into the third-story apartment, where I would share a room with my father who snored like a beast in the night.

CHAPTER 9

DOGS AND MOVES AND THE STRUCTURE OF MY LIFE

*This part's got to be poetry. For
the dogs if nothing else.*

And right now, as I'm writing this, my parents won't call me back because I told them I'm transgender, and they're taking it the worst out of anybody. We fought like nasty things after it settled in, and their logic in the fight was nothing of the values they instilled in me to walk this path. So, as I tell this next part just know I try to tell the truth and not skew the facts with vindictive fury. As poetically objective as I can. But if you see parts laced in razor wire, don't hold it too much against me. Cause I might still drive the four-door through their fucking house.

It started with Buddy in Philly, where I was born. He was a small, white mop mutt as most of them were, and I can't remember much else about that dog or about that first house in Mayfair other than spinning my belly across the coffee table and play-hiding from my dad when he came home from a shift on the force. Laughing and squealing, as my kids do now, he'd drag me from under the bed, scratching or tickling or almost hurting me with big, black, bristly mustache kisses. Those first few memories I have were real, real good.

What happened to Buddy, I don't know. We moved from the city to the Poconos when I was three, and Buddy, I guess, didn't make the move.

Rocky was a girl, and I can almost remember my dad bringing her home. He kept her in the crate in the trunk with the retractable trunk cover pulled over her for either purposes of surprise or to hide from the public that he could maybe care for a dog. We were far away from our house in this memory. Down by the road where the vineyard was, and that road came to a "Y" in a three-building post office town, and maybe one of the buildings was a diner, and we sat in that lot and heard her whimper and howl in the trunk and her nails skittered across the bed as my dad punched the gas and wound the three of us through the backwoods, me bouncing in the front seat all the way home.

John was scared to death of dogs. He lived a couple houses down and was the only boy younger than me in that little squad we had for a while. One day, I might have been five or six, Rocky locked eyes with John. The boy must have been a football field away, and he stood frozen in his driveway, unable to do anything but scream in place. Rocky likely weighed more than I did at that age, and as the boy screamed, the dog amplified and mushed with all her mighty drive and dragged me across the grass and over the modified stone headfirst like a water-skier too fat or too weak to pull himself up.

"Run, you idiot!" I groaned through the grass and the dirt in my face. It wasn't until she finally broke my grip maybe twenty feet away from the boy that the catatonic lock on his mind jimmied free, and he was able to scrabble on his hands and knees towards the garage door and slam it in my dog's face, nearly breaking her neck. You bet we heard it from John's dad later that night.

He was another bastard: creepy, stoic vibes of strange yuppy perfectionism. I remember his metallic blue Chrysler with soft, rounded bumpers and leather seats and smooth jazz playing to a man who gripped the steering wheel far too tight.

One time, maybe I was seven or eight, and John was six or seven, I tried to jump a fallen tree in their backyard with my bicycle and ended up smashing my genitals into the handlebars at full speed. The impact was so bad they started swelling up like a damn rhubarb. I dropped my drawers and began examining myself and cried and panicked and pulled my shorts back up and hobbled a half mile home, crying for my mother the whole way. Things healed and the following week I was back at John's house, only when his dad came in, he pulled me aside and questioned me on why I showed my genitals to his son. I remember looking at him in complete disbelief that an adult could be so stupid and so immature. To my mother's great credit, I think she told that man to pound sand in so many words. Her sharp Philly accent twisting expletive and shrill madness at a monied yuppy too disconnected by status to realize he had done nothing when her son thought he blasted his damn junk off.

Rocky had to go: I understand that one. She ate rocks and could break out of her pen, and we would lose her for days at a time. When she came back she'd be dragging deer limbs, likely from the corn field on the hill where they would go to die. She sits in my mind now like a weekend warrior, although I didn't know what that was then, with the blood in her mouth and that light brown crayon fur still stuck to the deer bone, just outside the sphere of satisfied and willing to relent because the animal in her was now finally exhausted.

Next was Mickey. Stallone was a big influence in our family if you haven't picked up on that yet. Mickey was a West Highland White Terrier we got from a breeder my dad's old lieutenant had married, who had also moved to the Poconos to get away from the hard memories of the city and general cop life. I remember going to their house when they had a new litter of puppies and I'd let them crawl, and scratch, and I guess subsequently piss all over me. And I remember thinking, "This is how I want to die," drowning in a litter of puppies.

We must have gotten Mickey at that first mountain view house. I know we had him at Uncle Rust's when we lived there for the three-month interim while we sold the first house and built the second mountain view house on the literal lot adjacent. I follow that logic too. That first house was too big. They overbought. My dad wasn't making squat in the Poconos because no one is making squat in the Poconos, and so they sold that property to a potato chip heiress, and they took me and Mickey to Rust's as they built the best house there truly ever was, the second mountain view house. That was a damn fine house. That much I have to acknowledge. And like all damn fine homes, it had both good memories and bad.

I can't remember why Mickey went. I think he was a ruiner of carpets. In my house it was less blasphemous to burn pages of the Bible for warmth than to waste a good swath of Berber.

Next was Sparky and we already know about that.

I had no dogs in that first apartment in Philly, but I had Barbara. Not to liken Barb in any way to a dog; I make the comparison only to elevate the status of my dogs to close friends. Barb was an early mentor at a time in my life that could have gone any which way. Barb was a diabetic, surviving twin who was overweight and joyous, and she lived alone in the apartment directly below us. She was a Black woman who worked for the prisons most of her life, and she allowed neither her weight, nor her health, nor her ethnicity serve her in any other way than expanding her brilliant mind. She told me stories of her youth, and most of them were about the public library, and we bonded over a mutual love of books and Denzel Washington movies. Her living room had a better VHS selection than Blockbuster, and it was always open to borrow anything I might want to watch.

Barb was such an interesting character in my life because, truthfully, I was closer to her than my own grandmothers. I love both my grandmothers dearly, God rest their souls, and I know they loved me, but there was a disconnect between us for different reasons and it just was the way it was. My father's mother was absorbed into the life of her daughter and my cousins, and their family was structured as the competitor family to my own. They were a materialistic lot with a Munchausen matriarch and a crossdressing father, and it was easy for my young mind to rope crossdressing up under the broader category of all other things evil and subsequently *not* Keiran. My mother's mother was mentally unwell, subjected to shock therapy and addicted to medical professionals. It's my diagnosis that she was something between mentally challenged and possessing narcissistic personality disorder. From my point of view, she was oftentimes too medicinally addled to connect with.

Although, if I might just lose myself down this stringy thought, one day me and Gram sat alone in the assisted living home where she spent her final years. Michelle and I had broken up for maybe the hundredth time, and she didn't judge her, and she didn't judge me, and there was a small moment of clarity in my grandmother's voice. She asked me, "Do you love her, Chuckie?"

And I said, "Yeah, I probably do, Gram." And she just nodded and hummed like she always hummed and maybe the thought went nowhere or maybe it stayed in her forever.

Then she looked right at me and said, "You know your mother loves you, right?"

I said, "I know, Gram." Then she offered me pills to help me sleep, but thankfully I wasn't enough of a scumbag to take them. Yet.

Barb would call me often, even after we moved out of that first apartment, and I would visit her for years. Every time I was home from college, I would visit Barb, and sometimes I'd be so tired from the constant drinking and the drugs that I'd fall asleep mid conversation with her. She'd just keep on talking at me, happy enough that I was back there in the apartment again.

The last conversation I had with Barb, I rushed her off the phone. I had just scored some primo acid and it was burning a hole in my freezer and I was aching for a "spiritual" experience, although I wouldn't know one if God Herself came down and punched me in the lip. I never talked to Barb again because shortly thereafter I was a complete alcoholic and drug addict, and I didn't talk to anyone. She died a few years later in the Camaro she treated herself to late in life, at a red light in northeast Philly, and I never even found out where she was buried. I intend to make amends for that. And so much more.

In that first apartment, ten feet above Barb's head as she read or maybe watched *Tomb Raider* (she really thought Angelina and I would be compatible), I would scissor sections of tank tops and make modified underwear and look at the girls in the Frederick's catalog, trying so hard to push this unrealistic goal out of my mind. But it never left. And like my altered clothing, stuffed deep in the depths of my dresser drawers, it too hid in the small cavities of my mind festering into what would later become a sepsis. I was thirteen years old.

We lived in that apartment until just before my first semester in high school. And that apartment was cool: a public pool, a dingy little chip and putt course, and some basketball hoops, and my dad would take me to all of them, and we'd talk philosophy and the heroics of great men, the importance of school and intelligence, and always...always, always, always...we'd talk about hustle.

Sometime in the fall, my parents purchased a twin back in Mayfair, a block away from the house I was born in. I could certainly not see the end product when I first walked through that house.

"It's got strong bones," my father said. But to me it looked like a dump. Not that I cared. I couldn't care less about hardwood or countertops or plaster walls "that really kept the heat in." I just wanted some damn friends in a school where I didn't have many yet. But I'd spend the weekends and the evenings sometimes helping my dad renovate the property, and I actually had some fun with him when he handed me a sledgehammer and told me to tear everything out of the kitchen. We would fart and laugh and eat good Philly hoagies, and joke in the mornings of the next day that our flatulence still lingered from the rip of the previous night.

And then one day in the basement my dad snapped.

"What am I doing?" But it was expletive laden.

"What the hell am I doing? I'm too old for this shit! I want to relax! I want to retire!" And he cried and he blubbered, and he threw tools and two-bys against the wall, and I just sat on those basement steps and watched him self-suffer. I can't remember if I said nothing and the devil just left him, or if I offered him words of encouragement. Let's assume I did say something to him because this wouldn't be the last outburst during the many years of renovated properties, and in those times my response could range from silence to rage to the invincible hope that only youth possesses. And so, my words might have gone something like this...

"What are you talking about, man? You're a beast. Who's more of a beast than you?"

To take my mother's words, "The world's not worthy to wipe the shit from your ass, Dad. There's no one like you on the face of the planet." And whether I said that to him or not at that moment, I know what happened next. He sobered, and the will of a Keiran took hold of the wolfish man. We played that first Chicago album, that one that still had all the magic in it, and worked into that cool, fall dusk. And I don't even think he washed his paintbrushes that night, which was an obsessive-compulsive ritual, and we drove on back to the apartment talking old cop stories and wild times of youth and madness. I think he even slept in Mom's room that night. And I almost couldn't hear the snoring through the walls.

Son of a bitch, that house came out damn nice. And when the renovations were done, but the itch of perpetual motion remained, my mom talked Dad into getting another dog. Rudy. A white-gold lab with a box head on him like a microwave, and he might have been the most beautiful animal I've ever seen in my life. Rudy was a hyper pup, like all labs, but his time with us would be evidence that big, hyper animals didn't last long in our homes of enforced immaculata.

Our time in that second Mayfair house was brief, and by the spring of my freshman year we had sold it, for a small profit, and moved out to the suburbs of Bucks County, into a small condo on a second story, and Rudy's days were numbered in that tiny spot. I can't remember, I think I went to Kenny's, or I was gone for a weekend or something, and when I came home Rudy was gone. My mom said he had nearly knocked her down the stairs and so they took him to a farm. And truthfully, I don't even think I felt anything. When I die, I hope I live out heaven on that farm where all poor pet choices go. Me and my wife and my kids and my dogs and the dogs of impulse Christmases, and the dogs of dead men, in the fields of eternity sleeping in one big, hairy pile of warmth and slobber.

Maggie was one of the best. That dog I think loved me more than any other dog, besides maybe Murph. She would get cold in the night because my dad hated the heat, and sometimes our bedrooms would drop into the fifties and I'd be weighted down in comforter after heavy comforter, and I'd try not to move too much in the night lest my body heat escaped. But sometime in the night when she would get cold, Maggie would hop up from the floor onto the bed and burrow under the sheets and sleep in the nook between my legs, and I absolutely loved that.

In that same condo, my dad retired, sort of. Our relationship became very close when that happened. My father was forty years my senior, and my mother thirty-eight when they had me. The year of my birth would also be the same year she would go back to school and get a nursing degree, spending her late nights and her early dawns nursing me and studying anatomy. And now my dad had "retired," and my mother kept working in a field she hated. So he got very nice, and she seemed very mean.

Sometimes in that condo, they weren't home; for a lot of my life, they weren't home. And truthfully, those were some of the best parts of my childhood. It was in those times that I could rummage through the one or two articles of my mother's clothing that I considered even remotely, modernly feminine. Or don one of my modified outfits and tuck a neck pillow up under my shirt like one big, singular fake breast. And then, I'd sit at my computer and play games, or do homework, or eat, or watch *Shawshank* or *Sin City* or whatever the hell else I had on DVD, and a lot of those hours were not sexualized, although that would come too, at times. Yeah, later on when my mind had ruptured, that would most certainly come too.

The sexual stuff, at first, came in imaginings and projections of female body types. I remember getting this video game for Christmas, Need for Speed Underground 2. It starred Brooke Burke as an in-game personality. Maybe one of the first games to do something like that. And I remember seeing her in her low-cut orange strappy top and her jeans and her finished nails thumbed through the belt loops, and I both wanted her and wanted to be her in some strange allure that would never leave. In life, I was very late to drink from the toilet that is pornography, and my earliest sexual fantasies were very innocent, and often materialized in no other way than fate producing some beautiful, Amazonian female on the television before me in the late nights, and I would rub my naked sides and feel almost female under the sheets.

I later found porn at around seventeen or eighteen, and I guess in some strange way it was meant to be, because until then I didn't even know what a trans-person was. I mean I did, but I never believed it could be so beautifully achieved. And even though I was first introduced to the transgender world in terms like "shemale" and "tranny," this unbelievable goal was being attained. That this title could be reserved for more than just the schizophrenic solicitation of those who inhabited the greater territory of the Art Museum or Market Street looking for handouts or the wizard who stole their brain. And although it was a world of degrading sex, it seemed maybe, almost possible. But I was terrified of being gay. In my all male, Roman Catholic high school with a father who would spit into the carpet every time Longshanks' gay son's lover got pushed to his death from the spire of the castle dour (we watched *Braveheart* a lot...like a lot, a lot), and from my experience in the Poconos, and from the greater life of the world beyond, being gay seemed so goddamn scary. And worst of all, I was attracted to women mostly, and transwomen, which my mind had always innately filed under "woman," and I needed no outside philosophical rhetoric to understand that. It's just that maybe being gay made more logical sense. And so the toilet would flush with each sexual release, and mount again in the coming days with the false bravado of brimming arousal, and so trans actions or trans thoughts could exist in that ruttish audacity only to be flushed again in guilt and grime for the next seventeen years of my life.

Maggie made a couple moves with us. After that second story condo, we moved to Richboro, another nice suburb of Philadelphia, to a property across from a golf course. The way my mom swung that deal was through the testimony of Mrs. Lawrence, a psychic from the days before my birth, who claimed someday my mother would live across from a golf course, and that she would be very happy there. Mrs. Lawrence also claimed that my mother's final child would be born a female, that she had visions of my mother braiding black hair, and so from my point of view I guess, *kudos to that, babe.* And we did live across from a golf course, but Dad left me hanging on that move, and it was Mom's strength that got us through that strange day.

Seepage pits. You may be asking yourself right now, what the hell is a seepage pit? Well, my friend, I could bore you with my doctoral knowledge on the flowlines of shit and its stages and its various destinations, or I can sum it up for you in the doctrine of smartass plumbers: shit rolls downhill. And don't bite your nails.

A seepage pit is basically a shit well of porous masonry that takes the spillover from your septic tank and gradually SEEPS it into the ground. Yummy. So why do we care? Because they're outdated and have a shelf life, and once they expire, you have to tear up half your property of redigested shit soil and install a modern septic tank system, and it's expensive as all hell. This fact didn't dawn on my dad until after he signed the closing documents on the property and his red Tacoma pulled into the driveway, the suspension scraping the road like a low-rider brimming with half of everything we owned. To the neighbors we must have looked like a white trash Sandford and Son, and I write that now with pride, because we were, and screw everybody else and what they think.

But he pulled into that driveway, and he got very quiet, and he stepped out of that truck and put his hands on his hips and stared at the garage that hung open in slack jawed stupidity from a chain motor with one too many links in it and the unsymmetrical wear of weathered hinges that only saw half of the morning sun tucked behind a palisade of off-center oaks. Then he did his act. He shook and he shook, and he snapped right there in front of my eyes, and I saw it coming before it even happened. And he left the truck in the driveway and took the silver Subaru and drove it up the road and beyond the golf course, and I spent the rest of the day unloading the truck and U-Haul by myself in another stupid house I didn't care about. It was all over seepage pits. Mitch, my brother, would buy that property from him, and it was one last sacrificial nail in the coffin of his personal bankruptcy, but really it was a testament to his immense class and his unspoken regard for the duty of family.

During the time at this property, I would date Kim, who would later become Tim, and maybe I had some small influence on his early embrace of that life changing choice, if for no other reason than my selfish meanness. Kim was the first person I loved, really. She had large breasts, but she was homely in certain ways. Although sexually we were happy to explore each other, I had a sneaking suspicion she might be a lesbian, and that suspicion was rooted, like all sneaking suspicions, in some sense of awful ostracization and self-hate. But she (because at the time when I knew her, she was she) was so damn cool. We loved skateboarding and movies and books, and we both wanted to be filmmakers, and she'd listen to my movie concepts and encourage me with every stupid plot to make the hard choices. *If you only knew now, my friend.*

Many years later, during the dark times, I would find her number. She was Tim now, and he was successful and in a relationship, strong and downright handsome. Our texts would read something like this:

"Hey Kim, or Tim..." *What an idiot I was.* "It's Keiran. How you been?"

And because he was still so damn cool, he texted me right back and the tone was happy and almost expectant.

"Hey, Chuck, how you been, man? We got to catch up sometime."

"Definitely. In fact, that's why I'm reaching out to you. I'm going through some gender issues, and I'm up against the ropes. I feel like I'm going insane. Maybe we could get a coffee or something sometime."

And I never heard anything from him ever again. The thought would cross my mind often that he might think I was toying with him. That news of his transition had reached me, and I was still as mean and cowardly as I was when we ended it. But a lot of people were letting me down then, and I wouldn't classify this as a letdown. Just Karma giving me a little of what I deserved. I was grasping so desperately for footholds in the well of life, especially at the time of that text message, but the mortar of the world was weak then, and chunks of sidewall just kept burying me alive.

I ghosted Kim, as they say, in the end. And she looked the best she ever looked when I did it, which was weird on my part. It was like she knew I was onto her, and so she came out tits-akimbo in this low-cut jawn with her butt in those jeans poked out at a hard ninety. It was the last time I ever saw her dress femininely because I would follow her, and watch his slow transition over the years, alone in the glow of my computer monitor.

I have two good memories in the Richboro house. One, Ivory Coast won its third game of the World Cup that year, and even though they were already eliminated, they went down fighting and that memory sticks with me still. And two, much more important, I kissed Michelle for the first time in her grandfather's Buick that bounced with the bumps in the road like a boat tackling choppy wake on our last night in the Richboro house.

Next, was an apartment or condo in Yardley, which was a rich section of Bucks County. I wouldn't call this spot particularly ritzy, but it was certainly my favorite of the high school homes. Dad went back to work because there was nothing to renovate in this place, and Mom was still working a ton, and me and Shelly and Maggie had the spot to ourselves, and Shelly and I would spend whole days wrapped up in knots in the bed and on the couch. It was the greatest time of my life, with the exception of the births of my children and getting sober.

We would ride this property out until the end of my senior year. College was a coin toss, and the only factor that affected my decision was proximity to my parents, so I applied to schools like the University of Hawaii and Oxford, and then ultimately Duquesne in Pittsburgh. I entered a contest that my school offered for those who got accepted to Duquesne because they were sister schools of the Spiritian subsect, and each year one graduating student would receive a full academic scholarship to the prestigious university. Fr. Jeff altered the course of my life when he awarded me that scholarship, and I'm indebted to him forever, but I know why I won that award more than any other reason. Because I wrote a letter so damn well, he accused me of plagiarism, and I looked him dead in the eye and laughed, and he knew then that he really did stumble upon something magical, and he gave me the award right then and there in his office. I've wanted to be a writer ever since.

The best part of Duquesne was that Shelly was going to the University of Pitt and we could stay together, which was phenomenal, but also I knew somewhere in me was a scumbag, and beneath that veneer, someone who didn't really know who the hell he was. That would be around the time I would recite this wicked mantra to myself.

"If Michelle ever finds out what you are, she'll leave you. You should just break up with her now, save her the agony." *But I can't. I love her.*

"Then enjoy it now, you freak, because likely someday she will find out, and she'll hate you like you deserve." Someday, she did find out. And she stood right there with me as I pumped myself with a thousand different concoctions. And carried me when I couldn't walk.

The summer before college, my parents thought it was time to move back to the Poconos. They were restless in the city. The fact of the matter is, we were broke. The fitters would love to twist my prep school education and my collegiate background like a corkscrew through my sternum and try to juice my heart they think might taste sweet with sensitivity, but the truth of the matter is we were more broke than any of their families were.

And, because we were broke, my parents couldn't find an affordable house that was anything close to the mountain view properties. I shouldn't say "broke." I never wanted for anything in my childhood, and my father avoided debt like the plague. We were working-man's broke. But throughout it all, through the good times, through the layoffs, through anything, my mother would never hesitate to buy me a book.

"There's always money for books," she would say. And they would be the best drugs I ever found.

That was a wild summer. I lived on the highway between Philadelphia and the Poconos, spent any money I had on gas, and set up a dresser in my trunk, so I could live out of my car for as long as possible, until I would cart myself the length of highway home and do my laundry and sleep in the basement.

This was also the summer I found booze. It was booze first, not beer. Vodka mostly, and that gang I hung around with then all had money, so it was glass bottle vodka, not that plastic shit, and I would spring up in the mornings like it was only the ambrosia of the gods that knocked me into slumber rather than soda and cigarettes and this new something that would pit my esophagus like battery acid and club me unconscious for only as long as my liver served as a sieve. And then I'd be up and awake for as long as I allowed myself sobriety. In the early days, it was nothing more than good, wild adventure. Thirty bucks split three ways, and we'd get bottles from the Mexican joint in Trenton that would bring the booze out back if you looked too young and overcharge you by ten or fifteen, and we didn't care because they were small heists as far as we were concerned, and the payoff was glorious consumption.

My parents lived in that Poconos property briefly, and for another reason I can't remember, they got rid of Maggie. They were moving into a fifty-five and older apartment building, and maybe it didn't allow dogs. My mom couldn't take Maggie to the vet where we left her, so she made me do it. I couldn't talk to that small dog on the drive there. My jaw clamped so hard up into my palate that if I did anything but breathe through my nose I might burst into a flood of tears. I hooked her to the leash, and we walked into the vet, and it was crowded as all hell.

I said to the girl at the counter, "I'm here to drop off Maggie." And she typed into the computer, and she said she couldn't find anything. Then she asked me what she was here for, but I couldn't answer. All the blood in my body pushed into my skull and I willed emotion out of my being, and I just shook my head at her.

And probably then she saw the tears in my eyes, and everything clicked. "Ohhh ... Maggie." I handed her the leash and I walked towards the lobby and as the glass door was closing behind me she said, "Do you want to say goodbye?" And I burst into tears in the parking lot and in the car. I pulled and punched that steering wheel so many times, I thought I might rip it out right by the roots.

I did college standing on my head. I was drunk or high all

the goddamn time, and the only decision of worth I made the whole time I was there was switching to an English major, which wasn't demanding other than reading a lot, but I liked that. Not that an English degree is worth anything. A roll of two-ply has served me more than a hundred-thousand-dollar degree, but it was the choice on a road less traveled. When the rest of the world bet along the pass line, I threw it all on the *yo,* and I still do, and fuck the easy road. I'm a writer, god damnit! I was a writer then, because I made writer choices, and I'm a writer now, in the basement near penniless. And if it's only me or my wife or one or two others who get to read this, then it was worth it. And I'll live out my noodle packet existence with the eternal happiness of the gutter-ape drunk sloshing in ecstasy from a few extra licks of the swill.

Sometime in my freshman year, my parents moved again. This time to a different fifty-five and older community, one structured as more of a trailer park than an apartment building. And so you could have dogs here, and they bought the exact same breed Maggie was, and named him Murphy, and Murph loved smoking weed. My mom kept Murphy in the crate during the twelve-hour shifts she worked, and he really only got to run around on those days for, like, an hour or so. My mom's drinking got bad then. I don't know why I hated her so much because she was suffering a lot, but hate is what it was at that time. I hated how far we lived from any reasonable highway. I hated that community and that trailer park home, and I hated all the old people there and their tomato gardens and their whispered words of past life victories. I hated the bar I worked at, and I fucking hated my boss. I hated that I was a drunk and an addict. I hated that I had an English degree and degraded my cashflow to a state that was worse than if I had skipped college entirely. But I loved weed. And I loved that dog, Murph. That was my man. And I was pissed when they got rid of him.

Murphy could not stroll through life, much like myself, and choked himself nearly to death when you tried to walk him for a piss. But on a run, he'd pace right along with you, in perfect gait, in perfect stride, and he'd look up at you from time to time, appreciative that you were finally keeping up and he didn't have to drag your ass anymore. But when we'd get out to the trees, to the little hidden area that exists in every neighborhood in the world, I would stoop down and light thin little swag joints and blow the excess in his nose and around his ears, and damnit if me and that dog didn't just groove our way home. Collars, both real and rhetorical, loosened and we just strolled home with our big, floppy feet slapping the blacktop heavy, and the world was bright and blue against fields of faded amber, and I never minded those moments. If they could just have lasted forever.

After all this, I was an adult and joined the fitters a year or two after this time. My parents would move another eight or nine times; I've lost count. And after Murphy there was Ben, then Rudy II, Yogi, and finally Lucky. It would be my greatest lie if in my hours of self-reflection, I didn't think all *this* was just the vengeance of an angry boy who wanted his fucking dogs back.

CHAPTER 10

MY BROTHERS AND CURAÇAO

Heroes. Absolute heroes. No other word can describe them in my mind. From the second I was born, I think, they would be set on that high pedestal for all my life, during times when they both earned the belt and lost it. They were always and forever heroes from wherever I stood looking up.

My brothers are fifteen years older than me, and although they are both technically half-brothers, I never describe them as such. Reg is my mom's child from a short-lived, failed marriage with Reggie's father, and from what I've heard, they both had their vices at that time. But Mom did the best she could. You know, the best that humans can do. And I'm sure she fell short many times, and I know Reg holds resentment in his heart even today, and nothing about those feelings isn't valid, and the only thing I really know for sure that came out of all that is that next to his wife and son, and Mom and my dad, there is no one else on the planet that loves that man more than me. I'd give him my breath if it meant I could hear his laughter one second longer. He's a damn good man and a damn good dad. And when I finally broke down and told him I was trans, he didn't blink and joked that the cause must have been from playing "pussy soccer," and I laughed for the first time in a very long time when he said that.

My brother Mitchel is my father's son. His mother was my father's high school sweetheart. But Dad ruined all of that through drink and neurosis, and would spend the next forty years of his life making up for it, and it's my humble opinion that he has made up for it. By twenty-seven, my dad would never touch another drink again. It would be too late to save his hold over Mitch and Peggy, Mitchel's mom, but his sobriety was soon enough for me. And although I witnessed a lot of the neurosis, I never saw my father touch a drink. Later in my life, when I thought putting a drink down would be an impossible task, I think I caught trails my father cut through the brush some thirty or forty years before.

Mitchel is the Man. I think that is the best way to sum him up in one word. A charmer. Handsome as true sin, even now as he presses closer to fifty. Age stabs at him like a knife, and I know he'll gloss right over that word if he ever reads this; it is the one reality he cannot morph with drive or cashflow. His sin is flash, and yet his generosity is his greatest attribute. Class. That's what he is at his best. True class. At his worse, well, I still love him. Even if I was just meat in the slaughterhouse and he the butcher's smile, I would bleat along the cattle shoot right up until that plunger was pushed into my skull. And if I know the man like I think I do, there may be a very convenient misfire at the cross section of my skull and the reticule and the pin that punctures the brains of calves. I might wake up in green fields, rather than prepackaged in cellophane kept cool enough not to rot, and hear forever echo through my mind the butcher's laugh and know it was his slick sleight of hand that saved a golden calf coated in nothing but cow's flesh.

Mitch was able to retire at thirty, maybe, with Reg coming up close behind him. In 2007, Mitch ran the largest mortgage company in Philly. Reg was the top salesmen, and when Mitch would disappear on weeklong benders, it was likely his step-brother that kept the bulk of that business afloat. I craved that so desperately as a child. I was smart, pretty objectively, and my mother hated that my professional aspirations couldn't extend higher than mortgage broker. Even my brothers tried to diversify my goals by encouraging law school. They'd say how valuable it would be to have a lawyer in the family and liken me to Tom Hagen from *The Godfather*, and I didn't know if they were sending me subtle signals to practice defense rather than business law.

But there was a disconnect. They were both fifteen years my senior. I lived in the Poconos for much of my childhood and saw them as frequently as uncles. But each time I saw them, their renown would grow in my eyes. A better car. A better babe. Girls that barely spoke English. Rolex watches. Shit, I think Reg even had spinners on that Lincoln Navigator, if only for a minute. And I just wanted to bridge that gap between blood relation and true brotherhood.

Then Mitch got two tickets to Curaçao. All-expenses paid. Free air miles. Free meals. And by the grace of God, he convinced my parents to let me go. And so we went to a Dutch Caribbean island a little off the coast of Venezuela. I was sixteen years old. I was dating Kim at the time.

Up until that point in my life, the furthest south I had ever been was Philadelphia. The furthest west, York, PA. The furthest north, New York City for a play we watched in a drama class I attended at the public school where Kenny and I went. Didn't even get a goddamn bagel. The furthest east, Cape May, NJ. Now if that ain't the vacation experience of every stupid Philly kid in existence, I don't know what to tell you.

The first thing I remember was the heat getting off that little prop plane. It didn't even pull up to a terminal. The runway was one grade above dirt, and we hunkered down from the plane on metal steps that were sharp and steep like a broken-down escalator and the humidity change compared to the artificial air of the prop and the Philly winter back home nearly choked the life out me.

The terminal, or the airport or whatever you want to call it, was overgrown on the inside. Jungle plants in pots left to coil out of their habitat and tongue the tile walkways and scrape along the grout lines as I guess that registered the most natural to the taste. The port was dead empty, except one or two people working the tickets and receiving baggage, and we stood out in the heat and flagged a taxi. I watched that same couple I had watched the whole flight push their mouths against one another and gasp for breath between bubbles in the other's slobber, and wondered if

I too might get laid on this trip.

Everyone that mattered spoke English, but this was not a primarily American destination. And when we got to the resort, the staff told us that our luggage had been lost, and so all we had were the clothes on our backs, which were not exactly the most stylish. We went to the gift shop and bought very tight fitting, European style bathing suits, as it was all they offered, and "I Love Curacao" T-shirts or something equally touristy, and stepped out in our new attire not unlike John Travolta and Samuel L Jackson in *Pulp Fiction*: a couple of dorks.

I think we just stayed around the resort that first day. The place had a beautiful reef not far off the shore you could snorkel through, and I spent that first day doing just that. Mitch might have had a couple cocktails on the beach and slept. Sleeping was something he had taken to an art form. After dinner, we hit the casino, which was also attached to the resort. Legally, the place was all eighteen and older, but so long as you had a pulse and cash in your pocket you could do anything on the island. We gambled all night that first night, and learned a beautiful game we would hunt down back in the states for many years after: Caribbean Stud.

"How much you make an hour?" Mitch said as he ordered another Jack and coke and pushed an artificial plunger into his neck, as though he was bypassing his liver and injecting the caustic serum directly into his carotid artery.

"Five fifty."

"Well, you just made ten hours of pay in two minutes." And we laughed and high fived and even I had a light beer that first night.

He could barely walk home that night, and so I carried him much of the way. And he said all these great things I always wanted to hear. That I was "pretty damn cool" and that he was glad he got to go on a trip with his brother. And I was never so happy in all my life.

The next day, maybe he felt bad for being drunk, but I didn't care. I had been awake for hours by the time he got up, and when he found me on the beach, he said, "Let's go rent some jet skis."

And I said, "Hell, yeah."

So there we stood in our shorty shorts and our tourist T-shirts and mounted these jet skis that had speed limiters on them, and my brother slipped the guy some cash, and the guy disconnected the limiter, and said, "Just be back in a half hour."

We went far out into the ocean and jumped each other's wake and rode those things to their near breaking point and then Mitch said, "Oh shit, we went over." And he sped off back to the shore. Just then, my machine shit the bed and wouldn't go faster than a mile or two an hour. I was far off the coast and saw angry signals flash in my direction from the dock owner, but there was nothing I could do to make the thing go any faster. Eventually two men came out on a boat, and one dove into the water and ripped me off the machine, and part of me thought he might strangle me right there in the sea. I climbed into the boat and the man was able to reset the jet ski and speed it off back in the direction of the shore.

They didn't charge us any more, but they were pissed as hell, and told us to just get the hell out. As we left the dock, some self-righteous American mom-type told us how bad we made Americans look and then she glanced down at my privates and her mouth latched shut like the many jowls of Cerberus. We had ridden those skis so rough that my flimsy European bathing suit had lacerated every which way and my jangus was damn near hanging out of my shorty shorts, and I think I must have laughed out loud at such a perfect punctuation mark to American self-righteousness and prudism. I might have walked tall almost halfway to the cab before I wrapped my lower half in a towel we stole from the rental shop we had just burned.

Back at our resort our luggage had arrived, thank God. And I think we celebrated by rolling out right then and hitting the club next door, and somewhere between then and the club and a couple Jack and Cokes, I told Mitch I hadn't gotten laid yet.

"It's just cause you don't have a car. It was like the second I got a car, that's when I was getting girls." He signaled for another round, and he looked beyond the bar at two girls drinking something from Long Island style glasses, and I said I was good on this next round. Truthfully, I was always afraid to drink. Horror stories of my father's previous life came to mind, and genetics, and my mother telling me I had the gene. And she was damn right.

"You see them?" I saw them.

"See, I like to play the eyeball game." I couldn't stare people in the eyes for that long. Not those two random women. Not my father. Not even Mitch.

"Stare 'em down. Then a nod or a smile. And they're gonna tell you everything they're thinking by what they do next." Like all first-time gamblers or game players, we hit on our first bet. They smile, and Mitch signals them to approach, and to my complete bewilderment they actually come over. One's tall and thin and Latin and Dutch, and one's shorter and fatter but with large breasts, and looking entirely Latin and downright *islander*, whatever that means, but it was my brother's word at the time.

"Yo, we just hit big in the casino next door and we're about to pop a bottle of champagne. Have a drink with us." That wasn't true. I was down to my last twenty bucks. But the girls were smiling and whether they believed the line or not, they were sticking around, and their drinks were empty and so...alright!

Then Mitch palms me sixty dollars and whispers in my ear, "Go buy the cheapest champagne they got, and we'll bitch and moan when they bring it over and it's anything less than Moet." He was talking Spanish as far as I could deduce, but I had mangled free a few key words. Champagne. Sixty. Cheap. Bring. Moet.

"Okay."

And so I sprinted off, and my brother ran the gambit. The same gambit that would certainly tire like a well-worn joke from years of overuse. But still to this day I laugh through it, because it's two brothers spitting tired game to tired women, and I think the Egyptians carved hieroglyphics that tell similar stories into the walls of their monuments, and so it must be something archetypal and beautiful. And I know I wouldn't change it for one second of something different.

"Give me the cheapest champagne you got!" I screamed at the bartender who either didn't speak English or couldn't hear a word I was saying over the wretched house music.

"*Que?*"

"Champagne man! Cheapest champagne!" The gangster next to me laughed. And I looked at him and said, "Fuck it, bitches, you know?" And he laughed even harder this time and took his drink and walked away.

The bartender brought out Moet and I signaled to the table in the back, and it was sixty dollars exactly and the bet paid one to one.

In the end, Mitch started getting sloppy, but we got both of their numbers and escaped before he could screw it up entirely. I had a few drinks that night but never got drunk, and some wicked thought entered my mind. *Whiskey is nothing but good luck, women, and good times, and it's certainly nothing to be afraid of.* But that thought felt too much like blasphemy, and so I pushed it out of my head just as quickly as it came.

The next four days went a lot like that. We went deep sea diving and my mask malfunctioned sixty feet underwater and I almost drowned, but then I didn't, and it was fun. And if that wouldn't be a perfect analogy for my drinking and drug use, then I don't know what is.

It's the last night in Curaçao. We call the girls from the first night and they want to hang. We take them to the casino, and I split eights with the babe on my thigh and double on the ten and double on the eleven and clean up four ways, and the only thing that felt better than skating the rake that night was the way my brother looked at me at that moment. Like I was his kin. Mr. Papagiorgio, he called me, and if it had ended right there it would have been a great comedy in the story of our lives, but it didn't.

The girls took us to this club that was more of a locals spot and one of their friends ordered a pyramid of vodka shots that we helped to deconstruct, and I remember telling myself, "It's okay, get drunk; we're having fun." Then my girl said she wanted a round of dwarfs and the whole party got quiet at the suggestion of such a hardcore intoxicant. And the tallest and baddest babe of the bunch ordered a round of dwarfs and I watched my brother's hundred get gobbled up and spit back out in the form of tiny cauldrons of bubbling froth.

"Put your hand over the smoke," she said.

"And swirl it around." I swirled.

"Then peak a little hole in there and sniff it all up." And I took a deep breath, and I don't remember what it smelled like but when I breathed again the whole world flexed in my vision and I swallowed the remainder of the drink in one big gulp. I looked at Mitch and he faked the drink and shook his head like I shouldn't have done that, but it was too late. Whatever was in that drink, be it drug or otherwise, I was straight mangled. Not sloppy. But a step or two behind my actions. And so on a trip where I had primarily steered the direction of our actions, now my brother was in control, and he was drunk, and we must have done something to screw it up with the girls, cause now we were outside, and my brother was lecturing me on the etiquette of foreign cabbies.

"You ever want to find the whores, you ask a cabbie." Did I want to find the whores? I got in the cab.

"Where's the spot, bro?" And the cabbie smiled. Those perfect white *islander* teeth.

"What spot?"

"You know the spot." My brother said and he lit a cigarette and passed one to me.

"Yes. I know the spot." And off we went.

The sign said Campo Alegre. No Food. No Drink. No Weapon. Parking at your own Risk. And then it must have said the same thing in Spanish next to it.

It was a campground of pastel painted longhouses of eggshell yellow with roofs the color of red clay. And there in the center of it all was a great purple open-air bar, where throngs of semi-nude women clung together in little cliques that seemed entirely determined by what shade they were. Some tall, light skinned, blonde haired Dutch types. Some short and fat and Mexican by arrogant American description. And then these strange looking hybrid women, all different heights and electric eye colors, and it looked like maybe God had nodded off onto the palette of their creation and rolled over and from his vomit and from his sin gave birth to Curacaoan whores, and left them on this mountain top to sleep with underage boys for forty dollars a half hour until death could set them free.

Mitchel was like a kid in a candy shop. But I was hesitant. Didn't stop me any, but I was certainly hesitant. And before I could fully put the brakes on, two of them grabbed us and led us by the fingertips into a room together, and Mitch pushed one by the throat onto the bed, and mine put my thing in her mouth.

When I saw my penis again it had a condom on, and she pulled me over to the same bed where my brother had already started mounting his woman. He choked her and maybe slapped her, and she said *"Tranquillo!"* Just outside the border of nervous.

And I said, "That means relax."

And he said, "I know what the fuck it means." He did not relax.

This scene was very complicated and at one point the woman that was with me reached over and started massaging my brother's junk while he still mounted the other girl. And my brother looked me in the eyes and cocked his fist and swung wide and called me a faggot.

"That's the chick, dude!" But that instant blinked out of his mind just as quickly and he was back to doing what it was he was doing.

I had good control. Always have, always will. And with the turn of a switch in my mind, I allowed myself to finish and got out of there just as quickly.

Mitch found me by the bar coming to and nursing a Red Stripe. He asked me if I was up for another round and I said no, but he wouldn't have it. He was too drunk to finish and so felt compelled to live here until he could vanquish the beast inside him. He brought over a different woman and paid her right there in front of me and she took me to her room and asked what I wanted, and I said, "Just a back massage."

So, she started with a back massage, and I think the *Price is Right* was playing on the little twelve-inch TV with antennas, and I shook my head as stupid overbid after stupid overbid gave the take to the one smart enough to just bet a buck. When she moved down towards my junk, I just stood up and said, "I'm good, ma'am," and wiped whatever lotion she had on my back off. That was the easiest forty bucks she probably made that night.

I'll never forget what my brother looked like to me then.

Strolling out of his little shack with his arms around two women, so piss-drunk and so cocksure, and I think if I hadn't stopped him he might have kept walking like a fool right off the top of the mountain. We made it back to the resort, and when we got there, I washed myself for two hours. At that innocent age, I also felt bad about the women. But I'd be lying if I said I didn't feel dirty too. Mitch slept all the way until the evening when we had to leave to catch our flight.

We turned our room keys in at the concierge and had an hour to kill before taking the cab back to the airport. We slipped dollars into a poker machine, and I blindly kept betting all-in because my mind was so far from that filthy slot. And then the thing cracked loudly, and four hundred dollars spit out, and I hit a five of kind on jokers wild, and my brother whooped loudly, and I didn't even react.

We had a layover in Bogota, Colombia. And while we were there, I heard our names pronounced again and again over the loudspeaker incorrectly, and I told my brother, and he said just be quiet and keep your head down.

We made it to the plane and sat down for maybe a minute and then two armed guards with AK-47s came on board and asked for "Keiran," and my brother stood and whispered to me, "Shut the fuck up, and if I don't come back, get Dad."

He never told me why they pulled him off the plane that day. And for the fifteen minutes he was gone, I thought I'd never see my brother again. But then there he emerged, grinning ear to ear, like he did it again.

And I said, "What happened?"

And he said, "Nothing."

And we've never talked about it since.

Before Mitch and I split at the end of that trip, I asked him, "What if I get an STD?"

"You wore a helmet, right?"

"Yeah, I guess."

"You're fine."

But I was a little Catholic boy who had his first sexual encounter with a Curacaoan whore, so I must have willed into existence the evidence of an STD. And now I had to get to a doctor to check it out. And my parents held the damn health insurance card.

"What do you mean?"

"I mean I think I got an STD."

"How?!" My dad was pissed, which was weird cause I thought I was picking up subtle signals to sneak away for some private time with my girlfriend then, but I guess in the end he was a dad and was supposed to be pissed.

Now I wasn't no snitch. Never have been. Never will be. Well, until the publication of this book. But whatever, get over it, all of yous. I know I am.

"Ah, at some dance. Some chick with a car. Drives me home. One thing leads to another."

"This didn't happen on that island, did it?"

"Are you nuts? You really think Mitchel would let something like that happen?" They looked at each other, unsure.

The doctor looked at my stuff unimpressed.

"That's a pimple."

"No, on my wang."

"Yeah, that's a pimple. You can get pimples anywhere." Then he took his glasses off, and snapped the gloves from his hands, and I walked in that eternal snap like maybe God really did answer prayers. Although I would never hold up my end of the bargain, and would get right back to sinning, maybe even later that day.

Some weeks later I would be at the mortgage company, and it would just be Reg and me.

"Yo, man, you hear about Curacao?" I bragged.

"Yeah."

"You hear about everything?"

"Yeah," he said, and he didn't look happy, and I was very confused that this great adult action didn't bring us all together. What I would find out later is despite Reg's vices, he didn't like that, at least not at that age. Reg was a father then I think, and his expression looked torn, between pissed and maybe hypocrite.

Years later, during the downfall, before I bumped into my boy with the coke at the titty bar behind the chemical plant, I was itching and Reg passed me some crystalized molly and said, "Fuck it, we never did shit like this together."

And I said, "Hell, yeah!" And I slurped that crystal up like it was icing and we sat there bumping Biggie, pulling off the pen vape back when they were a hip novelty.

Then he said, "Listen, dude, I love you, alright." And I told him I loved him too. And then we went inside, and coincidence crossed paths with my coke boy, who was more than that, he was my friend, but our strongest commonality was ripping gaggers and jabbering on about women and welding and rig work and money, and his coke was stepped on in the club and that only wet our whistle for decent shit, and before we knew it we were back in the northeast banging three hundred-bags opening up the Monkeys in a blizzard at seven AM drinking Jack and Cokes like serum refined from the fountain of youth.

Then I pinballed off a cab for an hour and half ride home in a blizzard, and I had nothing back at the place to help with a comedown off of whiskey, molly, and cocaine. And I'm sure I was on anti-depressants then too. I'd crack and call Michelle, whimpering in the harsh light of a midday winter, and although at that point in our lives she likely wished me dead, she answered and said it was okay and calmed me down and talked me all the way to sleep.

Sometime later in the day Reg would call me, and he said, "You get fucking goofy when you drink." And then he hung up, and I had to deal with those words rattling around my head for the rest of the night.

Nooner Or Sooner

CHAPTER 11

ZEN AND THE ART OF SHUT THE FUCK UP, OH AND WELDING

What a bullshit book that was. *Zen and the Art of Motorcycle Maintenance.* Hell of a title though. I hope any of the philosophy I inject into this book is incomprehensible. Not because of something stupid like my faux intelligence but because it's the lovely ramblings of a truly mad person. God, I love shit like that, don't you? When you release the structure of the mind and listen to the monkey's chatter. What great things are said. If you practice it, you can teleport. As real as a dream. Just be careful where you do it. Because if you blast the three-quarter inch nipple off the hydrofluoric acid line with a wonky piece of eight inch you're trying to thread through a rat's nest of miscellaneous gas pipe, not only will the shit eat through your skin and bone and stop only when it's bubbling with your marrow, but then after they saw your fucking arm off and douse you in soda ash, you're going to have to piss in a cup, and then they'll really have you by the nuts then.

That tank farm nightmare had ended. And I guess because I was still standing marginally upright and hadn't pissed Garvin off enough for him to physically strike me, I stuck around. Luke and I even got the old band back together and the three of us spent a winter in a chemical storage facility far upriver, tucked under an armpit neighborhood of fentanyl-addicted zomboids. To think that only ten years before, little old ladies would sit on their front porch and watch their grandbabies play and holler carelessly through the streets. All that being said, I hollowed free a few golden nuggets out of this otherwise deplorable shithole.

The facility's maintenance was under the management of a newly hired CA who had just retired from the Air Force. The man was both a complete gentleman and person of lifelong government employee pace, and so this became a lovely toilet to both hide in and refine my welding skills, as we had the time and lack of oversight to get down to *real* learning. When no one of value was present, Luke would let me stick weld carbon steel joints, and he'd stand over my shoulder muttering proper technique into my ear all the while. *You're going too slow. You missed a sidewall. You're long arcing. You're too cold. You're too hot. Slow down! Speed up. Stop fucking up!* But ultimately, he'd encourage you, like any good teacher does. And measured his own skill by how well he could get my joints to look, and by the end of that winter, they were looking downright decent.

"Who taught you how to run that 7018?" he'd ask me.

"Art Collins."

"Yeah, I like that! I'm gonna steal that."

And I'd regurgitate my observations back to the man, that not only was I able to produce the desired effect, but also translate what I was doing back into the English language, which is actually pretty hard for welders who have been doing the task unconsciously for so many years.

"Yeah, he runs a shoelace pattern. With an arc length just tight enough that the light starts to fade. And once he gets past dead man's curve, he goes up another ten amps, at least, and welds that top half scorching hot, and it makes it all look like a beautiful symmetrical weave."

"Yeah, I love it," he says. "I'm going to do that. Hell, that looks better than mine." It's those types of compliments, so rare in this business, that live on forever in a young welder's mind, and if I wasn't writing this book, I'd never utter it aloud, and dirty the small sanctity of the master and his apprentice.

--- - --- - --- - --- - --- - --- - --- - --- - --- - --- - --- - --- - --- - --- - --- - --- - --- - --- - ---

"I got a nightmare for yous, gentlemen." Garvin lit a Parliament, and I reached my hand out before he could put the pack away, and so he cocked his eyebrow at this kid who was getting WAY too comfortable bumming all his smokes.

"You mind?" I asked.

"I guess not. A two-inch steam coil froze and ruptured in the base of a chemical tank."

I wish I could remember what chemical it was, but I just can't. All I can remember is that this place housed the really nasty stuff. Nothing that will melt you alive like it will in the refinery, but it will eat you from the inside out, and years later, rotting in a leukemia ward, you'll wonder why you just didn't call out on that day the crew had to enter a benzene vessel, or whatever the hell it was. Think I'm exaggerating? George Frances was alive and well and a few years my senior and making us all laugh back on that first job. Before I got out of my time, five years later, he would be dead, leaving behind two beautiful children and a wife, because he spent most of his time in the refinery, and benzene is a nasty motherfucker.

So, it was Luke and me and two tankies, which are a subsection of boilermaker that specialize in tank and vessel repair and construction. I guess the plant figured since they were forced to drain all of their precious product, they might as well do some general repairs on the tank itself while it was down. I was fearless by this point in my career, having been lifted upwards of two hundred feet in a man basket to the top of a flare tower back in the refinery, put under fresh air, which is basically scuba for being in chemically saturated atmospheres, extinguished a small underground cavern fire that conveniently never reached the eyes or ears of safety, faked a few piss tests, and the list goes on really, but I wasn't about to play around with invisible chemicals that suck the breath of life out of you just when you finally start making money. Needless to say, I was sufficiently masked up before I entered the manway of this tank. The tankies were already inside, masks tossed in the chemical dust and debris that collected along the walls, smoking cigarettes and playing music on a small Bluetooth radio that sounded pretty awesome within those stellar acoustics. Every steamfitter in the world would be lying if they didn't look at the scene and think, a little smugly mind you, *that's why they're tankies and we're steamfitters.*

The welds were about an inch off the ground, and nothing ever breaks on the easy side of the pipe, so Luke and I had to bathe in that dust on the metal floor, grinding and welding the underside of a joint we could barely fit our tools under, let alone see what it was we were actually doing. But the man never bitched. So I tried to adopt the trait, at least during my time with him, and when frustrated take a second, breath, and then get my head back in there. It was Luke who taught me you need to approach hard joints like a puzzle and mold your body into the necessary shape required to see and semi-comfortably weld the joint. By the end of every one, you had figured it out; it was just having the awareness to remember that for the next nightmare that waited for you eventually, or immediately, depending on the job.

Winter thawed and spring came on us muddy and wet, and the three of us finished up our time in this placeholder chemical plant to head back out to the far reaches of our territory to begin work on yet another pipeline pumping station job. Tolls and gas could devour a young apprentice's check, but at least I had another guy from my class to bitch to about how much it was killing us financially to drive a two-hour commute each day. A-Aron would become one of my great friends in this business, although over the years he would voice his concern about the "tranny crisis" in the school system, and I'd just volley back my standard, "Yeah that's nuts," and deflect to some recent debacle from my personal life to get us off the subject and back to something we both agreed on: that we were both two big bags of shit.

He had anal sex with a woman he picked up from a bar one night and used olive oil as lubricant when she couldn't find her trusty bottle of Astroglide. That pretty much sums the man up in one sentence. But he had honor on the job, he was no rat, smoked with the best of them, and hated bullies. He could also work his nuts to the bone, so as far as I'm concerned, he shone golden despite his occasional scumbaggery, which we could all fall victim to at times.

Allen Fournier would eventually join that outfit of misfit toys. I would be quoted many years later saying to the occasional young, haughty, maybe college-educated apprentice, "They shouldn't let you out of your time unless you've done one job with Big Al Fournier," as he was one of the most notorious *apprentice breakers* in the business. He looked like the mutated offspring of Ronald McDonald and Howard Stern and preferred being compared to the fictious clown over a *heeb*, his word, not mine. He was insatiable and downright annoying at times, certainly bipolar, and there was a distinct difference in the man you could detect first thing in the morning if he went off his *medicine*, whatever that might have been. He could leave you in tears. Be that the actual rage-filled emotional breakdown of a person who just couldn't take it anymore, or genuine gut-wrenching laughter. He would never allow an apprentice any victory, even if he was right or downright witty. Worst of all, he was extremely intelligent and knew the trade better than most of us, and so he was usually right. He referred to me as *Poop*. And I laugh now remembering the days I hated him so much.

I would be lying to you if I said the man didn't rent space in my mind during my off hours. Scheming at ways to best him both mechanically and comedically and each nightly plot destroyed by yet another old trick he pulled out of his sleeve. Eventually I remembered my time with Luke, looked at Fournier as this puzzle that needed solving, and slowed my quick to anger reactions. I stopped fighting so much, and started going with the flow.

Everything was a *jizzilator* to the man. That's an industry-wide nonsense word for literally anything. Philadelphians would recognize the synonym *jawn* as a similar all-encompassing word. If something was a *jizzle-jawn*, then watch out, cause that shit's probably fucked up. There were two-by-one concentric reducing *jizzlators*. Long and short radius *jizzwoppers*. Three-weld, odd-angle *jizzballers* that ninety off the fitting make up to a riser *jawn*, and *jizzilate* somewhere on the pad and bolt to the outlet of the *jizzilheimer*. It was every part of speech, when required.

But more importantly, it was an all-running, never-tiring joke in the man's mind, and my greatest advice to a young fish out of water apprentice thinking of breaking into this business is to learn your audience. Quickly.

He had me down to one question per day. That was industry-based or personal, but he never really entertained many personal questions other than to tell me once over a chicken sandwich that he "didn't do very well" after his brother died, which he believed was from chemical exposure somewhere at some time. When he said this to me, it was like staring into the eyes of Richard Kuklinski, you know the mafia hitman known more affectionately as the Iceman, and he went to some very dark place in his mind that only a scantily clad mother of two munching chicken nuggets could rip him from. So I could ask him one question per day, and other than that it was encouraged to keep my mouth shut, or by his suggestion my "lips wrapped around the shaft of supervision." Either way speaking was discouraged, and what we had to listen to all day was whatever made its way over the lips of a highly intelligent insane person.

He was calculating the overall length of a run of pipe while subtracting various breaks and pieces of equipment that fractured and complicated an otherwise linear run. His final number was slightly off.

"Lobsterman fucked up!" His mood swings could break the sound barrier.

"You forgot the side-to-side takeoff of a concentric reducer on the run that breaks up the hill towards the pig launchers," I told him, and he flinched.

"Good catch. Okay, Poop. You're allowed one additional question today. Go."

I must have already reached my daily limit.

"Okay. I have to fill out this hydrostatic pressure test paperwork for the DOT. How do I calculate the internal volume of an eccentric fitting?" If there is one thing he liked about me, it was my intelligence. That a question to reach a little outside the limits of what is taught in the apprenticeship could even be formed in my mind was evidence enough that I wasn't a complete stooge.

"How accurate does it need to be?" It was almost the voice of a human.

"Fairly accurate, I assume."

He thought about it.

"We'll use calculus. I'll show you on paper when we break for lunch. I'm sure there's an app or some bullshit that does it for you, but that won't teach you shit."

"I assume, nineties and forty-fives are calculated by the radius length? I was just gonna…"

"Pooooop!" he interrupts me.

"Right. One question," I say, and by now his neurosis would just make me laugh.

"Okay, so we were off by the distance of a side-to-side measurement of a concentric eight-inch reducer. Now we add that to our number, take off the filter, account for the riser, and all that will give us proper…"

"Jizzilation." I finish his sentence for him. His miserable mask cracks, and I actually caught sight of his teeth through a smile he was trying to suppress. I was figuring this puzzle out, and maybe somewhere very deep down, ALMOST making a friend. I asked him one time if he'd rather bang the hottest *tranny*, sorry but at the time I used the word, in the world or the ugliest biological female. He spat into the ground and said he would rather kill himself. I don't know why I asked *him* this of all people. I guess I wanted to test the waters of the deep end before I went toeing around in shallower, safer seas. I concluded if he knew I was trans, or non-*jawn*ary, he wouldn't even look at me. You know a fitter really hates you if he doesn't even bust your balls. And that's a sad fact.

But he didn't know that about me. Shit at that time, I don't even know if I wanted to fully admit that about myself, but it would be coming and with it a terrible storm. But for the time being, we almost got chummy.

I've mentioned pigs a few times in this book so far, and to the uninitiated, you may be asking yourself, what is a pig? Well, there are all different types. You got your mandrel pig, solid cast pig, foam pig (the most common), spherical, and smart pig. I'm sure there's more but I haven't encountered them. Basically, they're a butt plug-shaped Nerf material (usually), ever so slightly larger than the internal diameter of the pipe they are inserted into, and they're primary purpose is to scrub the inside of the pipe clean of debris, rust, slag, and whatever other foreign material may have found its way to the inside of a pipeline. They can run for hundreds of miles, and are tracked and accounted for by sending the occasional "smart pig" through the line, which has both a GPS function housed within it, and some other scanning device capable of detecting any internal damage to a pipeline that would need to be treated as an abnormal operating condition and repaired. They are inserted into the pig "launcher" and caught at extreme velocity many miles away at the pig "receiver." Thanks to those principles of hydraulics, only a light amount of pressure, say fifteen psi, was required to push the pigs hundreds of miles through the pipe. If they weren't caught at the receiver, and say some weird section of pipe needed to be remedied of water, sometimes they would be caught in a backhoe bucket from an open flange, and I surely doubt there is any written procedure allowing this because it was rather unsafe, but what were we going to do? We had water trapped in an underground section of the pumping station.

Somewhere in the station the pigs got trapped, as they sometimes do, but rest assured they always jimmied themselves free; you just needed to be patient enough for physics to do its job. A five-hundred-year-old skeletal engineer stood by the open flange end of the pipe where the pigs were to be caught in a backhoe bucket. He put his ear to the pipe like he was tracking the hoofbeats of Custer's army. I saw an incident waiting to happen.

"Hey, uh, man. You might want to take a couple steps back because when that pig loosens, you're going to get blasted." He ignored my plea for both his safety and current dryness and just kept on listening like he doesn't speak to the help, and I quickly filed him under typical engin-idiot who never leaves the office and encounters real world scenarios.

Then Fournier puts his hand on my shoulder and whispers,

"Shhh. You did all you could do." And so we took a few steps back and watched the ancient relic get blasted by brown slag water once the pig eventually dislodged, which it always did. I tried my best to hide my laughter. Fournier on the other hand exaggerated his practically right in the man's face. Garvin took one look at the two of us and I thought he might have a stroke right then and there as this engineer ran the whole project.

"Kid fucking told you!" He might have laughed for thirty minutes if for no other reason than to rub it in the man's face, and every time that engineer sopped by us, he would start chuckling again and say, "Fucking kid told you."

I was sober for this eight-month run since the "car towing" incident, and so hadn't missed a minute of time, and repaired whatever slight scarring I may have caused to my reputation. So, like any moron with any stretch of time sober worth recounting, I thought it might be about time to treat myself, and planned a weekend adventure to Boston with my high school friend Griz, to visit the only gay friend I had in my life, Tim Kelly. Griz would bear witness to so many libertine adventures throughout my life, and we would both agree after it all, that Boston was pretty damn tame by Keiran standards.

Tim was in an abusive relationship with a younger man who had demons so manifest you could almost see the visible horns. Also, Tim very likely had feelings for me since high school in one way or another, so the friendship had complicated undertones to say the least. Again, it would be a lie to say I didn't flick the string of this invisible attraction from time to time, especially when inebriated. But when he moved to Boston, with no friends there, I made it a point to call him often, to check up on him, see how he was, let him know I gave half a shit. You know, like the behaviors of an actual friend.

Also, to set the stage for this trip, Michelle and I were completely on the rocks. The woman is many things but an idiot she is not. If we were together before I left, it was purely because we lived in the same apartment and for no other reason. She would tell me a few years later that she hated me during that time. She said, "I loved you so much, always, but you were a monster when you drank." She thought I resented her in my first bout with sobriety. In some ways she was spot on, but looking back at it all now, I think I just wanted to destroy that perfect love between us and free her from the hell that would be life everlasting with me. Not to say my appetites weren't animal when I drank, and most of her instincts were correct. For those of you reading this two timing, allow me to confirm your deepest fear, she knows. They all always know somewhere deep down.

I drank on this trip for the first time in eight months, and although no spectacular debacle occurred, maybe Kelly caught sight of the monster taking over again, and we nearly came to blows on the last night in Boston. The night before I had come out to Griz and Tim as bisexual. *Yeah, that was it*, I convinced myself. This is all the result of a closeted bisexual man, in an industry that would attest often, "Suck one dick and you're a dick sucker for life."

For the record, I've never sucked a dick—maybe a handful of figurative ones, but never the real deal. Not knocking it, of course, but not for nothing I think I just heard my dad sigh a breath of relief. Point is, this is something maybe my conscious mind could digest. The trans infatuation, the crossdressing, knowing the step-by-step procedures of slowly changing one's gender, the endocrinology appointments I would dodge at the last minute, yeah, all that was just the behaviors of a closeted bisexual man. But it didn't feel right when I said it to Griz and Tim at that club in Boston, and it certainly didn't sound right replaying in my mind over and over again in the silence of that car ride back to Philadelphia.

Tim took the ride back with us to Philly to visit his mother. Nobody was speaking to each other because I had threatened to choke the life out of him right there in his apartment the night before, the smug bitch. And then I don't know why I said it, and I don't know where it came from because I've never uttered the words aloud before lest I give them life.

But I said, "I gotta tell you guys something. And...and I need you to take this to the grave with you." Kelly was rolling his eyes. If I had to guess, his prediction was that I was just gay, and so from his point of view maybe he forgot how difficult it is to come out to somebody and thought it was no big deal at this point.

"Seriously. You need to promise me, you won't tell a soul. Not your wife, not your boyfriend, not your parents, no one."

"Fine," they said in unison.

"I, uh…" It was so hard to get out of me. "I, uh, understand this may be hard to see, but I think I'm transgender."

And I'll never forget Kelly's response.

He said, "Really?!" Taken aback that his radar could have malfunctioned so minutely and fired his shot just inches wide of what I imagine was his prediction.

Then we got to where we were going. We hugged and then didn't speak to each other for a year. He was my only gay ally on the planet. And he let me suffer for a year. I transmitted a million hateful thoughts in his direction over the course of that year, and honestly admit, if I had seen him during that time in the flesh, I might have killed him with my bare hands.

The next day I told Michelle and entered this fugue state I could not wake up from.

CHAPTER 12

LIVING DEATH

There's never really silence. Always some small chalkboard screech of frequency. Be it breath, sound, or whatever is preprogramed into our cellular structure that keeps us clinging to life despite every conscious attempt at making it rest. It never stops. Until it stops. And once then, there's no one there to experience the satisfaction of its stopping. The end is an illusion as much as the start. All we have is now. And right now, I'm going to try to remember the really bad times.

In those days, I drank. It was a constant act now. The alchemy of functionality had left, and I drank away my conscious hours with a sprinter's intensity, stretching forth for some invisible distance that changed nightly, where the power supply to my waking mind could be yanked out and leave me toppling forward and skidding face first to a halt in temporary nothing. Sleep would feel like a small instant, what little sleep I got. A jogging forward in time, a place where the record skips. And when I woke up, I drank, because those sober moments felt like raining fire. Some terrible pit would well up in my chest and reach out and pull everything about me into it. But I could stave it off with drink. And if I could stay drinking, I could keep moving.

I coughed to life on the futon in the studio apartment a little pissed off I had survived the night before. The apartment was empty, save the door keys, which rested on the countertop, a case of beer by the door, a bottle of whiskey by the fridge, and a couple of lines doled out next to where the keys rested. I had a fresh pack of smokes and a lighter somewhere, which would at some point add a scattering of tobacco and ash and cellophane to the items of the room. Other than that, the room was an empty cage of rolled primer. Static if not for me pinging off the walls.

I opened a warm beer and slugged, running interrogation out of my head as quickly as it formed. Primordial questions of the amnesic mind I didn't want answered. *How did I get here?* Slug. *When's the last time I went to work?* Glug. *Do I have enough money for a bag?* Sniff. And I crack a window and smoke a cigarette half hung out of it because it's freezing outside, and you're not supposed to smoke in here. The walls are so thin I hear the girl next door stir her tea, and wonder what hellish recounting from the night before she will carry with her all the days of her life.

The shower stopped draining weeks ago. There's a two-inch pool of hair and sludge that fills the tub. Also, the light switch doesn't work, so I showered by a sliver of light from the "hallway," which was a square of flooring that connected the closet, bedroom, kitchen, and bathroom, but at least it dimmed some of my sentient awareness of this nasty footbath I stepped into each day. It was a weekday. I had called out sick now for about a week and a half. And nobody bought it anymore.

I could not get drunk off of beer by this point in my life. My stomach would reach volumetric capacity before my mind registered the blood alcohol level. And so typically, I would get two large bottles of pinot grigio, and a fifth of Jack Daniels, and I would pour two glasses, one of whiskey and one of wine, and chase the sips of whiskey with large swallows of wine.

I watched YouTube videos on the floor of that apartment, while I was microwaving a bag of wet cocaine. It was not working to dry the substance out, and although I thought it might be too much to ingest all at once, I was out of the dry stuff and so licked the whole bag clean like livestock at the trough. Then I started laughing hysterically at something I saw on the screen and turned my head and looked back at the futon and said to Dan, "That's some funny shit isn't it, bud?"

Dan was not in the room. The mirage dissolved as soon as the words left my mouth and a current of electric anxiety ran through me head to toe. I realized then I should not be alone with my-self, as the evidence was stacking up that my mental health was significantly deteriorated, and I was in no condition for any re-building attempts. So I went to Dan's place. He was working but left his door open always, maybe just for me, and likely expected me to be there when he came home from work at night. Plus, he had weed, and I never liked to go long without it especially in the heart of a coke bender.

Marijuana, alcohol, and an upper, be it cocaine or amphet-amine produced this new effect in me that was entirely different from the individual substances consumed independently. I was a functioning zomboid. Capable of operating motor vehicles (I'm extremely ashamed to admit), walking into convenience stores, and clothing myself. Worst yet, I was makeshift handsome and even got the occasional smile. That road was taking me straight to prison, or the mental ward, whichever came first, and all the while bulk America was smiling on, like *there's a straight shooter*.

I smoke cigarettes by Dan's rear entrance until someone leaves, and catch the heavy door with my toe before it can slam shut and lock me out for the rest of the blistering day. I stub out my smoke, and say a couple prayers walking up the fire exit stairs that Dan left his door unlocked. He did, and Kirby, his Welsh corgi, greets me at the door.

"Hey-oh, Kirb." That dog was our boy then. When I would crash on the hardwood floor, because Dan's apartment was as sparse as mine at the time, with nothing more than an old Fly-ers' towel for a pillow, Kirby would crawl into my arms and keep my core warm through the night. And he was a trooper, even if you kept him up too late, and never judged my actions, just like my great friend, Dan.

Dan had had the same computer password since we were col-lege roommates many years before, and so I log onto his com-puter, pack a bowl, and pour my glass of whiskey, and pour my glass of wine. I was out of coke, maybe for the best, but Dan had a bottle of Adderall somewhere around here, and I could usu-ally deduce his hiding spots with expert Sherlockian detection. I would just assume the condition of the man, and usually that would produce the hiding spot.

"Ok, so I'm Dan. And I'm drunk as hell, and I'm high as shit. And I think to myself, Keiran's gonna steal all my shit, where can I hide this where *I* won't forget it? What do you think, Kirb?"

I look around the room and start rummaging through the usual hiding spots, then I have to piss and catch an image of myself in the mirror. I look back at the monster and say, "Why won't you die?" And forfeit my search for the pills as an act of fate, and just pack another bowl.

I was awake most hours of the day during this run and would sleep for maybe an hour or two when my mind would short circuit and the screen stopped displaying images. Dan opens the door, and I shoot awake with my head hung off the side of his bed because I rested at the foot of it like a dog, since to sleep in the man's bed like a human didn't feel right.

He said, "Jesus, Chuck." He almost never called me Chuck. Then he let out one very long sigh and said, "What'll it be tonight, bud?" And poured himself a Makers over ice that I could tell he didn't want to drink. Dan wasn't a complete degenerate like me. He could throw down, don't get me wrong, but he could pack it up too. But he rode those days out with me, not with judgment or maybe even opinion, but with the wide-eyed reverence of a ship captain ready to weather out the storm to whatever end or go down sinking with the ship. And I love him for this still today. At that time, he didn't know I was trans, and believe he just scratched his head at this invisible thing that wanted me dead so bad.

"Did you go to work today?"

"No."

"When are you going back?"

"I don't know if there's work to go back to," I tell him. And that was true. I was still an apprentice, and I was AWOL for almost two weeks. I figured I had thrown it all away. There was no way the union would let this slide. All those hours welding, everything I'd learned, the reputation I'd built, spilt through my grasp like sand in a hand that grips too tight.

Then we watched cartoons and before I passed out on the floor, my head propped up on that folded towel, now in elusive drunken bliss, I thought to myself, like I think I thought most nights before temporary death: *tomorrow I'm going to transition.* I fell asleep with a half-drunk beer still in my hand and Dan must have snapped a picture of me right then and there, and sent it to me many, many years later, so I could remember all this. Somewhere in the night I sprung to life and drank the rest of every half-drunk glass in the room, smoked several bowls, and willed myself back into unconsciousness. When I came to again, Dan was gone along with that wicked thought I had right before sleep.

The only thing running around my head in the morning was: *Why did God save me, just to let me die like this?*

CHAPTER 13

THE MIRACLE

Let's go back, shall we? I'm back from Boston and so I call Garvin and take an extra day on the back end of the extended weekend because there's a lot running through my head at this moment. Kelly's voice lived in my mind now. *Are you going to tell Michelle? You need a therapist. Are you going to tell Michelle? Tell Michelle? Tell Michelle.*

"Babe?" I actually slept in the bedroom for once. By this point in the relationship, I was spending my nights in the basement on a recliner hidden behind the faux walls of a few silk tapestries, where I could hide in pornography and video games. She was lying in bed on her phone, likely not knowing what to think about me.

"I have to tell you something."

"Okay?" And she sits up. I never asked her what she expected at that moment. Maybe the worst.

"So, I know this is going to sound weird."

"Okay?" She stretches the word out with heartache.

"So uh, while I was up at Boston, I told Griz and Kelly I was bisexual."

"Okay..." I've said it before, she's no idiot, and I'm sure she's had her theories over the years.

"And uh, but, that's not entirely true. I know what I look like to the outside world. I know how I behave. I know this character everybody knows. Because I made him." Expertly, may I add.

"And uh, well, on the ride home, I told them I thought

I was transgender." Was that the crack of thunder I hear, or reality shattering all around me?

"Are you gay?" Most everyone's first question.

"No. Well, I'm attracted to women if that's what you're asking. I'm attracted to transwomen too. I guess you should know that as well."

Then she just hugged me, and we sat in silence for a very long time. Let me tell you something about this woman. The kid's resilient. I've watched life bat this small angel back and forth, testing the limits of her will. She could fall, but never stay down. She rose from the bed.

"Okay, I love you, what of it?" She looked me in the eyes when she said this, and I couldn't believe it.

"I love you too. I'm so sorry. For everything." And she looked very deep into my eyes to see if that was true. Reflected in those seas of crystal blue I saw an inverse image of myself, and it looked to be a very sad thing, and I'll never know what *she* saw looking back at her right then.

That day almost ended nice. We went out, we got something to eat, and we forgot about it for the time being. All the while I couldn't believe I was walking through a world where Michelle knew my deepest secret, and in her knowing she could still stand next to me, still be seen in public with me, the *monster* and the love of its life.

The next day I went to work and in the isolation chamber of a jobsite shitter, something in me died and rotted. *I can't do this. They'll never accept me. They'll eat me alive. Bad enough I'm a college boy. But a tranny faggot? They won't stand for that.* And I ran away that night into booze and almost never found my way out.

Over the coming weeks, everyone in my life would question what happened when I went to Boston as there was a clear and defined change in my otherwise cheery demeanor. Even Garvin.

"You knock somebody up or something?" he asked as I just freely stole cigarettes from him at this point.

"No, just thought it was a good time to start drinking again," I told him.

"Yeah, how's that working out for you?" Putting down a drink for any length of time is always a Moses-like sea parting to those who never could, and I think some part of the man felt bad that sobriety couldn't be achieved for longer than he knew it couldn't.

"Not great."

My mom thought I killed someone. Or aborted a baby.

"Please, Chuck. I'm your mother. I'm worried sick. You can tell me; did you kill someone? Dad thinks you killed someone." She just wouldn't stop badgering me. And broken and deranged, I relented. How I came out to my mother is almost comical now, but at the time Caitlyn Jenner was all over the news, and I figured that might be the only public trans person she knew of.

"Okay. Fine. You want to know? You know that Caitlyn Jenner? I think I'm like that, Mom." Radio silence on the phone.

"You're what..." Her reaction seemed worse than if I actually killed someone.

"Like that. Transgender."

"A transgestite?" Correct pronunciation of words was never her strong suit.

I'll never forget what she said to me right then and there, as it would be a great wound for many years after, but she said, "Do you think those people are really any happier?"

And I said, "No. Probably not." And I hung up and crawled into the basement where I drank myself to sleep.

Time is very distorted now in my memory. A weekend warrior emerged of the most vicious variety. I longed for Thursday night, as I could limp through Friday and stay annihilated until Sunday evening. The Devil must have caught wind of my momentum and brought a steady supply of cocaine into my life through various sources both familiar and foreign. And maybe worst yet, the Big Job was starting, and I was getting shipped back Down River to work six tens for the next ugly year.

"Wake up!" I'm in the basement and Michelle stands over me in half a rage.

"We're going to my parents today." What was it? Thanksgiving? Easter? Someone's birthday? Whatever it was, it was said to me in a tone that didn't sound like I could get out of it. My immediate thought was how I was going to get through this day sober? So we stopped at my parents' house on the way there, and I stole as many Ativan and Ambien as I could get away with without their noticing.

Once at her parents' house, I sat on the couch drinking beers from a kegerator her father kept in the dining room and slipped a miscellaneous pill in my mouth every so often, hoping for a high that just wouldn't come. Then she said, "Chuck can you take Steve out?" And she saw something in me that seemed dramatically off.

Steve is our Australian Shepherd, and I stand out there letting him roam thinking of how I could go for a cigarette about this time. Then something happens to the Earth. The ground bellies like a wave and whatever locks that ball joint in at the hip loosens entirely and I fall face first into the ground with the audience of her entire family watching me from the kitchen window. I had two thoughts lying there in the dirt as Steve licked my face. One, *I think I just broke my neck.* And two, *this is really gonna kill my buzz.*

Michelle is standing over me screaming at me, "Where's the pills?!" And she reaches into my pocket, and they spill into the dirt.

I move my feet and wiggle my toes; my fingers still move, and I conclude my neck must not be fully broken. I blink, and it's the next day and I'm waking up in bed back at the apartment, and my neck is killing me.

"What happened yesterday?" I have no recollection of the events.

"You almost died. How's your neck?"

"Fucked." I lean over the side of the bed in a fog I have never before experienced.

"What the hell were you on?"

"Stupid shit," I tell her. The correct answer is *suicide combinations.*

"I thought we were going to have to pump your stomach."

"How did I get up here?"

"Kristen and I carried you." Kristen was one of Michelle's best friends and she lived with us in a room down the hall. Two, one-hundred-pound, five-foot girls, carried two hundred pounds of dead weight up three flights of stairs. I wasn't even mortified. I was pissed I hadn't died.

"I've been awake all night making sure you're still breathing."

"Oh. You didn't have to do that. I'm sorry." A gibberish word by this point to the woman's ears.

Then I got up, grabbed my keys, and disappeared again. I still have a pain in my neck to this day as a constant reminder of how close I came both to death and paraplegia.

Back on the job, I was losing it. Snapping out over little shit. Sweating all the way through my Nomex so that even my project manager (that's the top bull) stopped me one day and said, "Chuck we're worried about you."

"Nothing to worry about, Jim. Just got a little flu."

The job was scheduled six tens, that means six days per week, ten-hour days. But I hadn't made a Saturday in months, which is sort of a disgusting act by fitter standards as those are time-and-a-half days, and really help to pad your pockets.

They sent me for a weld test as I could weld stainless thanks to Luke, and when I got looked out, that means failed by subjective visual inspection, by the Texas inspector for being nothing more than a Yankee, I just went to the bar instead of back to work. This is an act so shameful and contrary to the standards of our union someone should have been shipped out right then and there to hunt me down and beat my ass. That an apprentice was even being given a shot at making the big bucks was an honor, and to behave like a bitch when he got looked out like everyone else did is completely unacceptable. I'm not saying my reasons were right. This is just how it went down.

This went on for a heavy year. And each weekend I got worse. I had six grandmothers die on that job if my steward kept a record of my excuses for missing time. Michelle and I left the apartment and moved in with her parents, something nobody was happy about, but we wanted to save money for a house, and I'd set the alarm off in the night waking everybody up, too coked up to remember the code. How her father didn't strangle me in the doorway, I don't know. But the world was rapidly sundering around me, and I didn't care about the mounting evidence because I was more and more convinced death would be coming any day now.

I knew my yearly drug test for the plant was coming up,

and I did not want the anxiety of needing to fake another one. So I white-knuckled sobriety for the month before the test. I would change my clothes a few times per night as I woke up in literal pools of sweat. But I was showing up to work. And I was bullshit sober. And so, everyone was happy.

Let's talk about suicide, shall we? Over the course of time since I had come out to Michelle, and even before, she got me to see every doctor, every psychologist, placed on every anti-depressant chemically combinable, all in a desperate attempt to save this person she loved so much, but who couldn't love themself. I could write a whole book on the ineptitude of America's mental health system, but I'll just sum it up with this. If you're a doctor reading this right now, and you get to that question on your little questionnaire, the one after the question, "Are you feeling depressed?" The one that says, "Are you thinking about harming yourself?" Let me tell you something they don't tell you in medical school, and something you're too scared to uncover in this age of litigation mitigation. *Every person who feels depressed carries with them some notion of self-annihilation.* And if you're coward enough to go to sleep at night getting a "No," for that second answer, then they shouldn't let you cash your big checks.

Suicide is not just something you dive into one night. There's this line in the mind of the suicidal. One you tiptoe around weeks or years before the act. You skip stones into the abyss of it, and measure reverbs of its potential depth, but there is no sound in this place. You think about how it will affect your friends and maybe your family. How the pain will both stop and start if it ever occurs. Then you beat the shit out of the thought, and wait for it to come back stronger some days, or weeks, or years later.

I was leaving the bank after work, and when I got in the car, I looked at the feminine mannequin in the store adjacent. I could walk through a chemical minefield, swing from scaffolding like Spiderman at heights that would make the average person puke, weld in orifices so tight to take a full breath would mean breaking your sternum, lift four hundred pounds, and bout with the best of them. But I would never have the courage to walk into that store and buy something. And it was that realization at that moment on that day that I had finally crossed the invisible line.

I never owned a gun despite my father being a cop and knowing my way around one for the singular fact I was afraid I might off myself on one particularly bad night. Tonight was that night. I headed to the Dick's Sporting Goods to buy a shotgun and a box of buckshot, and I was going to shoot myself in the mouth right there in my car in the parking lot. On the way to the mall, I called my dad for some reason.

"Hey, man." I'm sure I sounded off. "I just wanted to tell you that I loved you, man. Alright?" Something in my tone choked him up. My dad did not know I was trans at this time. I had told my mom not to tell him, and she agreed it would wreck his already unstable mind.

"Why am I crying? What are you doing? Where are you?"

"It's all good, man, don't worry. I just love you, alright?" And I hung up the phone. I parked in the mall parking lot outside of the store and cried the hardest I ever cried in my life.

Listen. The bulk of this story is autobiographical fiction. I've taken liberties to protect myself and protect my friends and offer you something that will entertain. But this next part is all true. This all really happened. This miracle was real. And I need *you* to know that.

I looked at a wooden cross that hung from my rearview mirror. I had received the cross many, many years before from a high school mentor during a time when I was less of a coward. I gripped it in rage and ripped the leather cord that it hung from and through my tears and through my hate I screamed at the Almighty, "Show yourself! Fucking show yourself!" At that exact second, I received a text message. It was from Tim Kelly of all motherfuckers. The text read, "Did you know Griz is Jesus?"

I actually started laughing and said to the Lord, "Okay, that's actually pretty good." Then I retied the leather lanyard at the point of the break with a square knot that was stronger than the unblemished band itself. Then I called Griz, who at this point in my life often screened my calls, and maybe for good reason. He answered that day, and we went and ate tacos. And my brains remained securely within the boundaries of my skull.

And although God saved me at that moment, and I stayed sober maybe one more night, I would not take that yearly piss test clean, as the next day I was paid for something I can't recount in this memoir (be this memoir or fiction) with a thousand-dollar fistful of coke, and disappeared from work and the world and sleep for the next two weeks.

CHAPTER 14

DEPRESSION, ADRENALINE, AND THE LOGIC OF THE DAMNED

The second phase of the Down River expansion project was like nothing any of us had ever seen, both the green and veterans alike. Fitters and tradesmen were gobbled up from the world over to man a project reaching upwards of five thousand men, two to three thousand of which were Steamfitters alone. And so Down River became this maelstrom toilet flush, sucking into it every colorful character from every low-wage crevice this country had to offer and emptying ultimately inside the barrier limits of the Down River gas storage facility.

Six nearly football field in diameter tanks were erected over a two-year period of overtime. The tanks reached well over one hundred feet high and stored approximately three million barrels of propane, ethane, and butane, requiring over nine million man-hours to build. I was told that should one of these puppies blow, the blast radius was an estimated twenty-five miles, so at least there was no threat of feeling any of it. You'd be dead before you even realized what had happened, smoking outside heaven's day room still waiting for St. Peter's call when he said you'd be through the turnstile two weeks ago.

Down River was and still is a refinery town. Units occupy city blocks with high pressure gas piping bridging public roadways with a diner and bank and bar and other hard-won conditions of a long-inhabited prison. I was sixth period. I was a complete mental wreck, and well on my way to full blown crackhead. Had I wished to accept that title, the drug was readily available both inside and outside the gate.

The general foreman was a man named Marciano, like the boxer. In the summers, he wore cutoff jeans in the old man Italian style with the tips of his pockets hanging just out from under the fray of denim. He was close to retirement and so couldn't give less of a fuck about anything really. Just don't get hurt and smile, both of which proved quite difficult for me at that time.

We were to thread a piece of twenty-inch diameter pipe between a high voltage line and the erected steel bridge rack where the pipe would transverse a public roadway. The difficulty of it all was that the middle of the pipe and subsequent rigging point was roughly around the ten-foot minimum distance required by OSHA standards of high voltage wires and the rigging of anything in proximity to it. The work-around, so the pipe didn't seesaw unit-side, slip, and crush the men below, was that yours truly was to climb up into the rack, attach two chain come-a-longs to the bridge side of the pipe, and rowing-machine the heavy mass inch by inch until the fulcrum of that first steel beam was far enough to keep the pipe from falling out of the rack.

I signaled the crane via radio vocal commands as the crane operator couldn't see my hand signals where I stood tied off in the rack.

"Boom down, hold the load. Boom down, hold the load. Boom down, hold the load. STOP!" And the pipe stopped. I and the dogman out-of-town fitter who stood in the rack with me scratched our heads as the logic of this thread job seemed to be mostly fired from the hip and impossible without the usual, you know, breaking every fucking OSHA standard at the risk of our own careers in order to pull off a superintendent's "I told you you could get it!"

Then the pipe started tipping.

"STOP!" I screamed into the radio, but the pipe didn't stop tipping.

"JESUS, STOP!" I screamed again and the bridge side pipe end made contact with the insulated high voltage wire.

Dogman and I both flinched at contact. Nothing happened. But with each passing second the pipe tipped further into the tension of that wire and squeaked little high-pressure fissures into the insulation.

"UP!" I screamed. "Take weight! Take weight!"

The skyhook flinched up a fleck and the pipe froze. For a maybe a second, I was scared to wrap the chains around that pipe end, thinking the whole thing must be electrically charged, but shrugged it off as I wouldn't feel a thing should I get zapped out of the rack and plummet through the front windshield of someone driving underneath just hitting the high note of Whitney Houston's "I Will Always Love You."

I wrapped the chains around the pipe end and sprinted back across the rack, tying off from D-ring to D-ring with my double lanyard harness like webs shot from Spiderman's wrist with my precious Mary Jane in the clutches of that Green Goblin guy. Then I chugged those chain come-a-longs like a rower against the current of Niagara Falls, and pulled that pipe end down and off the wires and across the rack, inch by exhaustive inch.

After it all I stood in the smoking pen with dogman and the crane operator, none of us speaking. I'm not sure what those other men felt at that time, but I felt very alive for the first time in a long while and thought maybe I could solve all my problems if only I had a brush with death every day for the rest of my life.

CHAPTER 15

DETOX AND THE AFTERGLOW OF MIRACLES

I wasn't with Michelle anymore. And I couldn't stay in that studio apartment either. I was afraid of being alone. Afraid where my mind could go without perpetual distraction. Afraid of what I was capable of. I was just running scared, numbing any feeling that welled up inside of me the instant it formed.

So I lived on Dan's floor for two nearly sleepless weeks. Then one day, outside Dan's in the morning, I called my mom. She was sober now and spoke of AA and its benefits often. I figured the inevitable comedown waiting for me might get a little gruesome and decided to give in to my mother's incessant pleas for medical intervention.

"Mom, I gotta go to rehab." She agreed and thanked the Lord. To her credit, she called me back an hour later, saying they could take me in that day.

"Whoa, hold on. Tomorrow. Tomorrow. I'll go tomorrow."

Her voice cracked as she did not like the sound of that but appeased me, knowing she held in her hand this very skittish thing that might scuttle under some rock in the sand and no amount of digging would unearth it again.

"Tomorrow, at eleven, I'll pick you up."

I told her I was at Dan's and where he lived, then I hung up the phone and drove directly to the liquor store.

One last night of wine and whiskey. The Big Boy jugs were on sale, and I got two of them. And a Big Boy of Jack. And then two airplane bottles of Belvedere at the register for sentimental reasons harkening back to the onset of alcoholism many years prior when I hid bottles under my bed for nightly consumption. Then a sleeve of coke cans from the convenience store nearby and a fresh pack of smokes. Then I went back to Dan's. He was working, and I drank and smoked like I could see the *Enola Gay* breaking just over the horizon and my inevitable obliteration coming with it.

I'd like to tell you it was some crazy, riotous night, but it wasn't. It was solemn and quiet, especially after I finally broke radio silence and explained to my general foreman I needed to go into rehab. He was furious with me up until that moment, but put it all behind him and like a true fitter brother said he would try to spin it like I was on vacation, and maybe save my career in the process. He texted me later in the day and said they weren't buying it and that they had to lay me off. And I said I understood. Then I left a voicemail for the head of my apprentice program, explaining I had to go in for a five-day detox, that I wouldn't have my phone, and I would reconnect with him once I was out and plead my case for his mercy.

Then I called Michelle. I don't know why. That bridge was burnt. Scorched earth was all that remained. But she always answered the phone when I called. I told you she was an angel.

"Hey."

"Hey."

"I'm going into detox tomorrow. I don't know why I'm calling, but I just wanted you to know."

"Oh, Chuck, that's so good. I'm so glad to hear." And she genuinely was. I know she hated me at that time because I hated me at that time. There just wasn't much left to love. Dogs wouldn't even lick me; I must have tasted like shit. But why this fragile tenderness in her voice when I called? I offered for her the perfect weak spot to drive her heel into; why was she reaching down and scooping me up? I always loved her. I was just such a damn fool.

In detox, they would ask me what I consumed daily. I was

leery of telling anyone anything, and I honestly didn't know. There were no days anymore by which to measure. There was only awake and unconscious, and these times were not separated by any determination of Gregorian calendar or solar interval. And honestly, I didn't know how much I consumed in a day. I consumed as much as necessary to reach unconsciousness; beyond that it was all semantics as far as I was concerned. I told the girl a six-pack a night. She told me to stick out my tongue and counted its oscillations. Her expression said my count didn't jive with the tremors of my tongue. Her name was Sarah. And that's what I called myself, for a while.

There was some pill in there they could give you, to help with the DTs, which by that evening were starting to hit. But they must have forgotten about me, preoccupied by immature opiate junkies. I didn't relate to anyone in that detox facility except my roommate, Frank, who was a mid-fifties Black man who also worked the trades and figured he too would be out of a career when he reemerged from this facility. Also, I was foolish enough to not bring smokes and this man had brought them in abundance and shared with me and likely saved me from Kool-Aiding straight through the fucking wall. If ever I caught sight of a lost generation, there it was. Teenagers or young twentysomethings crying for their mothers or scamming or weaseling an extra of this, an extra of that. Don't read my tone negatively: if life presented a similar course, I'm sure I'd be doing the exact same thing. Maybe that was waiting for me eventually, it's just I still walked the tightrope of feeding my addiction with my own means with a job that paid halfway decent, instead of having to scam for it.

And I'm just shaking in silence in a corner, three Rocky movies deep by now, trying to not appear ungrateful for the general hospitality and shelter, when I see the nurses wrapping up shop for the evening.

"Sarah." She looked taken aback.

"Is there a pill or something for this?" I show her the tremors in my hands especially when I stretch them all the way out.

"Did you not get your pill when you came in here?" It came out of her with genuine concern. She was younger than me, and so monotony and misery had not yet stolen her zest for making real change. God bless her, I hope she's more resilient than the lot of us.

"No," I tell her, and she checks her books.

"Oh, man you got to be hurting right now."

"Yes."

"Why didn't you come up to the nurses and say something?"

"They appeared overwhelmed, and I didn't want to be a bother." Truthfully, I didn't want to appear like a junky and get some asterisk next to my name that said *cut him back on those quicker than most.* Naturally, I didn't see the irony in my logic.

She laughed and gave me the pill, whatever it was. I swallowed it there in front of her, tucked my hands back up into the nook of my shoulder, and limped on back to the room. I read the Big Book for a little bit, lying there in bed convinced sleep would never find me. The pattern of books seeking me out during my low periods remained consistent, and although I didn't consider it the next *Count of Monte Cristo,* I figured it was still a damn good book. Then, my roommate stirred one final time in bed and tore the universe partially asunder with some low, bellowing spatial anomaly that erupted from his asshole, both engulfing the room in noxious gas and shaking the plastic sconces on the wall. Like a prisoner about to be experimented on, with this nauseating cloud filling the room, your less than humble hero of this tale fell asleep for the first time in over two weeks and slept soundly well into the morning.

That next day was one of those rare gaps in the Earth's crust in which I could lay low, where tectonic mashing slots free a temporary crypt of refuge in an otherwise violent spectacle of shaved and shattered walls of rock against immense pressure. Outside of the sealed unit, my world was falling apart. I could make no contact with anyone, and if I thought about that too much, I would start pacing the floor with the endless well of pro-pulsion that anxiety produces. So, for that first day at least, I put my scheming aside. I ate a little bit. Smoked as many of Frank's cigarettes as he would offer, and in exchange taught him about the ins and outs of Steamfitting, and how his age, experience, and (for good or ill) race might actually benefit him in transferring into an Apprentice program. We exchanged numbers, and I encouraged him to call me once he was out, but they gobbled him up for a thirty-day rehab, whereas I worked weasel words to skate after the five-day detox.

Let me tell you a funny story about intelligence and mental health in our modern American society. Before I joined the Fitters, I was going to join the Army to be a Cryptologic Linguist. There was an immense sign-on bonus at the time, and the job offers after time served paid well into the hundreds of thousands. So, when I took the ASVAB, I scored a nearly perfect score, if not entirely perfect; I can't remember. Then, some almost fictionally huge master sergeant stands over my shoulder looking at the results on my screen and says to me, "Well, next was the Psych evaluation, but we can just skip that seeing as you scored so high on your test." And I just said, "Okay," and figured it best not to site counter references to Lex Luthor or Josef Mengele.

I told the guy who ran the place, "I think I'm just bipolar. Sure, I was drinking and drugging and I needed this lockdown. But I don't need a thirty-day rehab. If I do the thirty days, I'll lose my career, and if I lose my career and the last four years of my effort, no amount of amends is going to stop me from shooting straight over the bridge and dissolving in a fifty-gallon drum of fentanyl."

It's weird really. How scheming had somehow likely manifested into the truth. Lie long enough and you'll produce the reality of your fiction. The mind will retrace the story you tell, rather than maybe the one that really happened. *Are the forty thousand words behind that sentence the manifestation of weasel shit or are did they really occur?* The correct answer, like all correct answers, is *who gives a fuck?* And just *keep moving forward.*

The man who ran the place said I could make one phone call and arrange for a pickup tomorrow at noon. The call under his supervision naturally. So I called Michelle, of course. What other force than an angel could pull me from the pits of Hell itself?

And I say to her, "You don't have to be my friend; you don't even have to talk to me. Just get me out of here. I just don't want my mom to do it."

And she said she would be there. I would find out years later that Dan, my great friend, was pretty distraught over the whole thing and met with Michelle some time while I was in detox. There he pleaded my case, saying about the same thing I had said. "You don't have to love him. You don't have get back with him, or even like him. Just be there for him because I don't know what else to do."

And she did all that and more, and that Miracle in the parking lot of Dick's Sporting Goods was starting to gain momentum.

Frank was throwing a fit because they wouldn't let him leave. I don't know why, but he was cornered by three men and a sheet of paper that translated into a very hopeless look in the man's eyes. Then he looked past it all and saw me there with my bags waiting for him, and he said, "You go on and be good, brother. I'll call you. Steamfitter, right?"

"Steamfitter, bro. You call me, Frank!" I yelled over the commotion and that was that, as they say. I never received his call.

Then, in the lobby, there she was. I don't think I've told you enough about her to fully illustrate what I saw there before me. A word like "angel" generalizes her glory as if to only quantify her in color rather than the artist's impasto. She stood in that room like a canary atop a tinfoil organ, every subatomic movement amplified through the pipe mouth she clung to, and it all played this song of hope and despair and love and triumph that almost brought me to my knees in electric overture. Her eyes were the color blue like when the universe started, and her skin ethereal like maybe there wasn't even a skeletal structure beneath it, and it was the will of God alone that stood the woman delicate and upright. And she hugged me one of those good, tight hugs she gives, and I couldn't help doing what I always do and kissed her right on top of her head, as she so perfectly fit into place there.

Once in the car, I bugged. And said if I go back to that apartment, I'm getting in the car and just driving until I can't drive anymore. But then, some other thought was flung into my skull that jostled the coward stupid, and so I told her, "Take this exit here." This was the town we had lived in during some of the good times, and the start of the bad days, but there was a motorcycle shop here I would walk through on occasion and romanticize the day I could afford the bike of my dreams.

Again, let's talk manifestation. Many years before, back at the mortgage company, I would look at this royal blue, matte finish Triumph Scrambler every day, and tell myself, *someday I'll have this bike. No matter what it takes, I'm going to get this bike.* So, when I walked into the motorcycle shop on that day, I thought I was just going to ogle my bike one last time, then maybe forget about it entirely. But, Vince, the shop owner, said, "You know we just got one of these in, used, in mint condition from a vet who stored it *garage kept* during his deployment. Matte blue." Then he said the number and it was downright reasonable. I gave Vince a hundred-dollar bill and told him I would be back in the morning to buy it outright once I could figure out some financing method. And with no job, no money, no prospects, literally days sober, committing to an action AA would scream against, I bought my magic bike that kept me sober for many years after.

The following week, I met with the head of my school. I always thought of the man as firm but fair. I recounted my tale, glazing over the parts where I was a giant cokehead.

"Chuck, if we threw every guy out who had an alcohol problem in this program, we'd be unable to man our territory. Also, despite all of this, you are still the top of your class. And other than the most recent one, your work reports have been stellar on the whole."

Schoolhouse Rock whispered through my memory that *Knowledge is Power.* He seemed to chalk the whole thing up to boys will inevitably be boys, proverbially of course. I gave him my word that I would never drink again, and for at least the remainder of my time in the apprenticeship held up my side of the agreement. And he held up his and treated me like any old bag of shit apprentice that walked down his halls. I'm very grateful for that mercy. And I tell you that as testament to the occasionally equable disposition of union men.

He called me one week later with a job down at the airport, and it would be the greatest job I had landed in my career thus far.

A hodgepodge crew of brilliant maniacs ran both the airport maintenance and an underground stainless deicing line job that ran from a series of glycol storage vessels to a hose-down area where planes could have their wings deiced in the winter. Although the crew was manned with mostly drunks, the other apprentice on the job was just under one year sober and so I was granted an ally against the constant temptation. It was summer. It never rained. I rode my bike every day to that job. And moved back in with Michelle. And felt the light of the Lord shining upon me. And the universe opened to present opportunity after opportunity for me. It was truly a miraculous time. I attributed all of it to getting sober.

Sometime at Michelle's, my transgender identity came up, and I told her I didn't ever want to think about it again. I didn't want to talk about it. I just wanted to put it behind me, and focus on getting sober and strong. Physically strong, I got. I lived at the gym, and so would download evidence that a human body could be physically transformed through willpower and determination. With each polite "No" I got further and further away from picking up a drink, and felt a strange sense of invincibility I had not known since maybe I was seventeen. Funny thing about invincibility; it's the greatest delusion of them all. Be it through age, or indulgence, or the efforts of master villainy, you will lose the gift at some point and feel in you some slight pity for the next puffy fool that crosses shoulders with you on the street because you will know that they don't even see it coming.

I found an AA meeting that I could tolerate during that time and rode my scrambler to it regularly. It was packed with old heads and construction fucks. Bikers, whores, bus drivers, and general nutcases. I felt very much at home. And listened to their tales of woe and redemption, realizing then I had come so close to losing more, and here I was thinking I had already lost everything. I took all this in, through the good days and bad, and I won't kid you: early on there are more bad than good days. But then the scale starts to tip. Breakdowns become more sporadic. Over the gathering months, some semblance of a brain reformed, and there was a fog I was exiting. Yet I was so convinced I had given myself some permanent brain damage in those early days of sobriety. With the scale tipped and momentum building, I was gliding now. But what was that drag I felt behind me? A dark magnetism that said *this thing inside of you is not entirely slain.* Not yet.

I had said to my mother one day after an AA meeting that was weakening in its effect on me, "You know, Mom, this is all good, but I feel like all of this was a symptom of some greater thing inside of me." She brushed it off, and told me to brush it off. And so I did, and only sipped transgenderism through a straw at the high tide of ruttish belligerence, and then the wave would break back with shame and guilt as it had done throughout the entirety of my childhood.

After that airport job, Michelle and I got married, and I said I've got to stop with this trans bullshit. But it didn't stop. Then I had my beautiful daughter, Josephine, and I said I've got to stop with this trans bullshit. But it didn't stop. And then my beautiful son, Michael, named after one of my childhood heroes, and I said I've got to stop with this trans bullshit. And it never stopped. Try as I might, for thirty-two years, it never went away.

Early Quit

CHAPTER 16

MAKE ME A CHANNEL OF YOUR CREATIVE WORDS...

I pray to God every day before I write, and I put in these words all of my faith, and I need *you* to know, especially now, during these times of lost logic, that I believe with all of my soul and the rest of my bank account that a person can change their lot in life, no matter what they're from or where they're stationed. There are monsters in the dark, but rest assured, they're only coward things. Too petrified to wield their might in the light of day lest blank recognition disintegrate their terror. And so they coax you to the dark, and deliver cheap shot blows effective only on the blind victim. But here is what *you* need to know. They won't kill you. Bleed you near dry, maybe, but they'll leave the final act for you to finish yourself. And if you do it, just before you do it, you'll catch your first sight of light in such a long time that it might almost look like the real thing. Do not be fooled, it's only the sheen of their snarling grin, eager to finally consume you, knowing now definitely they had you in their webs all along.

When he finally snapped and told it to me *real*, because he said, "I know how you like it straight." He said what I was doing was akin to child abuse, and don't you want to drive a crowbar through the skull of a child abuser? Then he said he loved me, and I told him he didn't know what love was.

For many years, I harbored hate for them, it's true. But then the thought entered my mind, that the Lord gave me a million shots at redemption before I finally took one. Maybe people stumble along the way, but at some point, someday, they'll see the light. They'll let go. And they'll inch along the uncertain path of love, one that leaves your arms up and your kidneys unguarded. Life will jab you there in those tender spots, but just keep tumbling forward and know that that red slurry that pisses out of you each day is an indication of proper form and the right roads traveled. The roads we need as a whole people. The Kingdom of God is built in pissed blood and belly shots. Try to remember that when you're screaming for breath.

Now I want to apologize for starting Mom and Dad off as bastards in this story, because they weren't. They were parents. And like all parents they came equipped with whole lives of neurosis and regrets. But like all *good* parents, they shouldered it all as best they could, juggled what new horseshit got thrown onto their plates, and like any of us fought like wild dogs when they felt like the things that *should be* weren't. I didn't realize any of that until I started raising children of my own. And then the laughter of my kids unlocked a million happy memories I had lost in clinging to the shit ones. I think I was just mad for a while that they couldn't accept the same madness in me that was in them. And maybe we could be damn happy if we all just let ourselves to be crazy together.

CHAPTER 17

MARATHON MAN

In the mornings I ride ten miles one way on a blue Trek bicycle to the shutdown Down River, over the hills and through the hood and along a four-mile stretch of industrial highway. The whole job thinks I'm nuts, but they love a good nut. By the time I get there I feel fully warmed up and shoot the shit with the gate granny who can't figure my extra effort out.

I tell her, "Schwarzenegger says no zero days, and I got the marathon coming up. Gotta be ready."

"You're nuts." She says it like three generations of the woman's lineage spoke it at the exact same time. As though things *goofball* were so preprogramed against her DNA, they are as impossible as human levitation. Not for nothing, but I still on occasion try to float a few inches off the ground.

Once through the gate, it's straight to the tent. It rained last night, so half the thing is torn and flooded, and mosquitos have started a breeding sanctuary where we eat and rest throughout our extended twelve-hour working schedule. I have the hellish title of job steward, liaison between the whining of both the men and supervision. Three guys already stop me to complain before I even reach the Nomex trailer.

"Stew, you gotta do something about this tent, man. We're gonna get fucking malaria." It's Pop Pop, designated job old guy, but don't let that fool you: he outworks most and he's slicker than any engineer I've ever met.

"I told the Cheese about this a week ago. They ain't gonna

do shit. Fuck it. I got an idea." I step inside the tent. Morale is at an all-time low despite my best efforts to promote a steady stream of degenerate gambling, killer tunes, and sneaking the kid out on Friday and Saturday mornings to get the men breakfast from the diner.

"Yo, fuck this tent!" I holler over the general malaise and sluggish shuffle of men getting ready in the morning. "Take over these trailers next door. They were supposed to be for supervision, but fuck em. This is ridiculous. Big Fat Paul is already over there. If anyone gives you shit, tell em the stew said it."

I hear someone from behind the lockers shout, "The Stew of the NORTH!" And I can't help but laugh. On these jobs you're miserable, but you laugh all day long. Just like a good life lived. There was a faux schism last week after BFP accidently ate a fly that landed on his breakfast sandwich, and so he declared himself Stew of the North and withdrew from the tent to claim real estate in the trailers reserved for supervision. Who's going tell a four-hundred-pound angry welder, whose breakfast sandwich just got ruined because of poor job conditions, that he can't sit in their trailer? Hades himself would flinch at a hungry BFP.

So they call me the Stew of the Seven Kingdoms, and half the tent slug over to claim a spot in the trailers, dragging their cushy computer chairs and gear behind them. I stay in the mosquito sanctuary. I prefer the limited seclusion I can afford in a day. I'm trying to finish *One Hundred Years of Solitude*, because it's on every greatest-books-of-all-time list, but it's not for me. I didn't have a big family.

It's Monday, so before we trudge out to the unit there's a safety meeting outside the tent where Safety and Supervision tug on themselves in front of the whole job and publicly fluff the few turncoats who blow them in discretion. The bulk of the men, regardless of trade, stand around in a circle trying not to vomit or explode or drill their eye out with a quarter-inch drill bit. But at least it's a reprieve from the start of the day.

The talk of the meeting is a faulty alarm system that had been causing unnecessary evacuations all last week, and when the meeting concludes I start taking money on a *closest without going over* bet for when the first alarm of the day will blare. BFP hits it within two minutes and I'm sick because he's been hot all job and I'm already down a grand on this shutdown. Franny Scott tells me he almost lost fourteen grand over the weekend, but the Patriots broke him even in the last play of the game, and I tell him, "If I lost fourteen G's, if I didn't shoot myself my old lady would."

The compressor building screams at a decibel level so loud that it can almost push you backwards, so I climb the barrel ladder in the rack behind the building as quickly as I can to get above the noise. It's a beautiful late September day and the Wolverine is already up here with good tunes blaring from the makeshift weld tent we'll spend the next twelve hours of our day in. Not saying the best, but we were likely the fastest Tig welders on the job, and so they placed us on the *critical path* welds, which were the most paramount welds to complete before this shutdown could progress further. Top brass would poke their heads in constantly throughout the day to see how far we were progressing on the joints, and the Wolverine would dial back a few inches per hour every time they did it out of spite, and I loved him for it. Wolfy came from a non-union background and *cleared* the apprenticeship because of his phenomenal welding skills. He was loyal and had balls and so was turning out to be a great union man.

"You're not going to like this, Chucky."

"What..." My heart sunk and I turned up the radio.

"Nightshift welded out that first joint without splitting the difference on the second."

"Jerkoffs!" I say, but I can't blame them. I'd probably do the same in their position and hit them with a real sincere *sorry* as we pass each other at the gate.

We had a thirty-inch tee we were cutting into a butane line to divert some of the gas to a newly constructed compressor pad that the rest of the job was working on. But the tee was at the top of a candy cane of pipe and so there was no linear or vertical play in the lines, and what you had for plum and square of the joint faces was what you got. Our initial analysis of the situation was to split the difference between both mismatched joints, so they both bear a medium amount of difficulty, rather than one be a layup and the other a completely wretched nightmare. But nightshift took the layup, and left us with a full court buzzer beater to contend with.

We just stared at the joint in silence for a while thinking and motherfucking. The gap on the bottom and at *dead man's curve*, which was about four o'clock on the pipe where most of a joint's difficulty lay in a 5g production weld, was enormous. Almost three quarters of an inch. Standard gap on a pipe this size is about a quarter inch, which accounts for inevitable shrinkage as you would weld it out. We spend the first few hours of the day doing everything in our power to come-a-long the gap tighter. It doesn't budge. There's no place for it to give.

Then I say, "What if we just weld it as is, but we start at the top and work our way down? Tying into our starts with every few inches we descend? And as the weld cools in our descent, the gap will squeeze tight, and God willing by the time we reach dead man's it's more manageable than three quarters of an inch?"

The Wolverine thought about it for a second. Then he said what all great welders say, "Yeah, fuck it. What choice do we have?" And I smile and turn the radio up real loud because Motley Crew is playing and there's still some latent neural pathway in my head that associates *Livewire* with the dopamine release of cocaine.

And that's what we do for the next twelve hours, work our way down this nearly unworkable joint in positions of agonizing yoga-induced stasis that require me to rest my head on the scaffolding from time to time because my neck muscles are just about giving up. In the blink of an eye, the day turns to night, and we're all but buttoning up dead man's curve when the welding inspector rushes up the barrel ladder to tell us we need to go home for the day, and Wolfy and I look at each other, and think the same thing without confirming it between us verbally.

I try to politely explain to the man, "What would you do if you walked into your shift with a five eights gap on dead man's waiting for you?" And he okays our extra innings right then and there. After fourteen hours we get a root and a hot pass in, almost to the applause of the inspectors and night shift alike. Night shift now gets the sweet juice of just filling the rest of the joint up. Anyone privy to the game knows that was a damn hard weld, and no average schmuck could backfeed a gap that wide, not with the eyes of ten *jits* on them at least.

It's dogshit black as we badge through the gate, and Wolfy asks if I want a ride home since I rode my bicycle into work that day. I tell him I appreciate it, but I'm good, and jam my headphones into my ears and start peddling through the nightmare town that is Down River. It was something out of Stephen King's *IT*, and I was watching for balloons to start inflating out of the sewer gutters. I rode far onto the shoulder and mostly on the grass when I could as I traversed the industrial highway home because of the low visibility but felt surprisingly welcomed as I peddled with the other long-haired white folk through the hood. Difference was, I was just trying to get home and not score a speedball.

Back in the house finally, after riding twenty miles on a bicycle and working an insanely physical fourteen-hour shift, I microwave whatever Michelle has waiting for me in the fridge, and sit on the couch in an exhaustive high not unlike a good drug. I fall asleep on the couch. Today was Monday. And I have seventy-two more hours of work to go before the next one rolls around.

After the shutdown, I would linger on with this contractor and work eight to ten hours of plant maintenance per day. Once complete, I would drive to the city's art museum, park my car, and run eighteen to twenty miles every third night in preparation for the upcoming marathon. I had never run a full marathon yet by that point in my life, and wanted to do it by thirty, as it was something I set my mind on, and I've always been testing my powers of manifestation.

On the day of the marathon, it sleeted a cold, wet, steady misery that actually felt good on my joints, and I think the weather helped me finish the race. The last mile was grueling. Nothing muscular at that point, the pain I felt was mechanical. My hips were screaming, and my ankles had long since seized up, and I cracked and wobbled across that finish line, but what I felt there—to the congratulations of no one—was not some great sense of victory or accomplishment. It felt more like I had spent the last few years running *from* something rather than towards it.

The next day I bought a big bag of high-potency marijuana, smoked the biggest blunt physically rollable, and heard screaming in me a thousand ancient voices that I just couldn't will dead.

CHAPTER 18

RESPITE AND THE TORTURE CHAMBER OF THE MIND

I say this next part delicately, and understand, please, I mean no offense in what I say, but the Pandemic was the happiest period of my entire life. I understand the world was and still is suffering from its effects, but for me, it gave me a three-month reprieve from my hyper-masculine working environment to write, and think, and explore a life different from the one that engulfed me. Plus, my son was born the week before the world shut down, and I got to spend the first three months of his life all day every day with him, and that time was the most pleasant turmoil of my life.

This is a common experience of all steamfitters and maybe all tradesmen—or cops, or firemen, or nurses, or EMTs, or armed service personnel—anyone who works prolonged hours, but it always takes a few days after the shutdown into the layoff to reassimilate back to normal society. Yes, we drive the same highways as the *normal* mass of humanity. You'll see us in your grocery stores, at your local banks, but in our minds, we're still back on the job. Fighting invisible battles. Beating invisible bolts. Plotting offsets for complicated thread jobs through murderous product lines with a crew that's half brain-dead and half brilliant. Halting f-bombs midair as they spit from our lips in the faces of clerks when all we really wanted was a can of dip and a howdy-do, and not really a *fucking* Skoal. The attitudes and behaviors of the life are sticky things. And it's hard to turn it off with the punch of a clock and the rotation of a turnstile. Now try to make the change from Sly Stallone to Cindy Crawford in the forty-minute drive through traffic with modest success and your mental stability still intact, all the while the *motherfucks* you fling out the window at the guy who cuts you off sound distinctly masculine. Play that mental game of tennis five or six days per week for over a year *testing the waters*, and tell me if your hands don't shake when you try to steady them, and that your eyes can stay focused on one target long enough to pull the trigger. It doesn't matter if the symptoms manifest or don't, I'd call it a victory so long as you're not mostly adorned in tin foil cutting down 5g signaling relays a day behind the guys that just installed them.

The point of that is, it took me a minute to *feel* her. To let her inch out of me in a world that mostly hated her existence, and I no better than that world. And once out and once properly decorated, it would be words from my mind that would beat her back into her bestiary. I had to let Michelle know that she was still alive in me. And my wife never blinked. And she always loved me.

So, I get a therapist, and at first, it's hard to even say the word *transgender* aloud. And I sing the timeworn chorus of closeted trans folk and their miseries. There are days of progress and there are days of setback. I cry about the difficulties of the job, the reaction of my parents, the reaction of my friends, walking down the street without clobbering to death the first dirty glance I encounter. But with each day, I'm further away from that thing of perpetual movement everyone loved so much on the job. I'm certainly no beautiful creature during these days, but I duck the ropes of a mental bout that is surely destined for the full distance, and for the first few rounds get the absolute shit pummeled out of me.

During that time, I collect a few articles of clothing, dial sex up to a redlined eleven, ping back and forth between *I'm doing this,* and *I can't do this* every hour on the hour until the world tells us we can all go back to work.

Once back, I'm sure of it. *I can't do this.* I make a poorly executed joke about fellating a baker as a result of a bunt cake's addictive quality in the men's trailer and you might have thought I spit on the flag. But why can't I get her back in her cage? She's tasted the light of day. She's felt love. She's felt sex. Life isn't all bastards and blackness. There's a world worth living through here, sometimes? And I feel it in me. She wants it. She wants me to want it. But I'm fighting her. And she me. We're tearing apart this body that houses us, and smoking ourselves stable.

Over the year since the pandemic, I inch just a tad further into the light and twist our experience together as much as possible before I peel her away and tear whatever grafting has taken place. Because then I make a choice...

...I buy a rig. I buy a new Chevy 3500 HD with a utility bed in workman's white with no bells and whistles, but I buy it new because I'm not a gearhead, I just know how to drive the things. Then I put a Lincoln SAE 300 HE on the back of the truck and I bolt it to the bed, and I put two reels for leads in the rear driver's side utility box, and two more reels for an oxyacetylene hose and a remote reel in the driver's side box over the wheel well. Then I park the thing in my shared driveway, walk inside the house, take an Ativan, and cry my eyes out there on the living room floor with my wife and children watching me the whole time.

And I said to Shelly, choked out between each exhaled sob and inhaled whimper, "I was so close."

She rubbed my back and I said, "I was so close to transitioning. I never got this far before. But now I have an eighty-thousand-dollar rig payment in a bad economy, and these Texas inspectors don't want to pass straight white Yankees because of the placement of the Mason-Dixon line, let alone long-haired trannies, and I can't sit on forty hours with this payment, and I sure as shit can't live off of unemployment anymore."

And then I cried and I cried and I said, "What did I do? What did I do? What did I do?"

And Michelle said nothing, and I could feel her pain. And Josie said, "Daddy's sad."

And then I said, "I'll be okay, baby." And I was. I told Shelly I'd take it one day at a time. That the fight wasn't over yet. Financially, it all felt like the right move, but nothing I did felt like *flow*;

whatever that bullshit word means that calms unexcited hippies and aggravates the already prickly logician.

--- - --- - --- - --- - --- - --- - --- - --- - --- - --- - --- - --- - --- - --- - --- - --- - --- - --- - ---

If I may digress for just a moment, allow me to confess one innate prejudice I cannot remedy despite my best efforts at self-reflection and sublimation. Texas welding inspectors. I don't know how Texans claimed the monopoly of weld inspection nationwide, but some big belt buckled supervillain must be twirling his mustache, spurs on the table, pulling the strings of some larger welding inspection governmental agenda. Before I lose myself down the very evidenced-based theories of Sith-like infiltration throughout the national pipeline weld inspection racket, I'll just offer the counterclaim that Texans are perhaps the only people bred boring enough to pride themselves on the ripple symmetry of a bead pass. Now, I know that sounds almost derogatory and maybe even plum prejudiced, and I just want to assure you that it absolutely is. The hellish torture inflicted by Texas welding inspectors on welders of my territory, and myself personally, has created a Magneto-like vendetta against the larger mass of the entire state. I encourage, regularly, the secession of the state from the greater union, as we can finally remove the state as America's disfigured bulge, and relegate Florida as the country's new shriveled penis (although they're on thin ice too). I sincerely apologize if *you* now are reading this as a resident of Texas. I'm sure you are a fine human, and nothing of the despicable nature that spawns a potential weld inspection career, but I am willing to sacrifice you entirely for the necessary remediation of the larger infection. Mushed mouthed one-upmanship about how great your state is, how poorly our unions are run, how big your dicks are, tits are, mitts are, and overall greater jitload quantity, how much better the sun sets in Texas, horseshit smells, blue jeans feel, proper missionary technique, and a completely unflinching belief that whatever it is that is currently exiting your speakhole is one hundred percent indisputable fact has driven me to near totalitarian round-up methods, and all I can offer in defense is to assure you the end is truly worth the means. (Naturally I tell this as a joke and wouldn't sacrifice *you* for the world. Unless you're a Texas welding inspector. Then may you enjoy the many jowls of Lucifer's ultimate torture, you fucking homunculus.)

So, I come out to my friend, let's call him Drax. We had been friends since high school, roommates in college, and now we're both steamfitters of the same local. He is the only person in this business I can TRULY trust. A pipeline project was coming up, and I figured I needed an ally to, maybe quite literally, watch my back against whatever reaction could be expected of Texas inspectors. I had my rig, and if I could squeeze by the welding test then I'd get the pick of the litter as my helper. And seeing as I intended to tread deeper waters with my transition, I figured Drax might be the only ally I could afford at the time. For the sake of the truth, and to illustrate the immense, all-triumphing power of true friendship and brotherhood, I need to tell you a bit of what kind of person Drax is. Drax is self-admittedly a bit of a black-pilled conspiracy theorist, leaning mostly to the right side politically, and to the objective eye reads like someone who wouldn't associate himself with topics transgender. He never blinked. Best of all he didn't change one aspect of his behavior in respect to me or our friendship, and that's really all I wanted. He's still just as insane as ever, and me with him, and his loyalty and friendship are something I will never forget or abandon.

But that was it, I broke the seal. I came out again. And felt a bit of that fugue state almost four years behind me then spread by muddy osmosis through my walking reality. Shortly thereafter, I came out to Michelle's family, which is sort of a sad thing because I came out to them before my own father, but at the same time was this very tremendous thing in that their reaction was nothing but love and acceptance. Then I came out to my dad, and my parents' reaction was okay that first day, but by noon the following we screamed at each other for several hours straight. It was a rough road. Me and Mom and Dad. I think all of us bashed our heads against the concrete many times. It's seldom written about, but this is one of the pathways to enlightenment. Some small glimpse of it. Do the things that drive you to bash your skull off the concrete floor. At some point you won't want to anymore, either the things or the bashing. And what remains is what always was. And wonder what it was that drove you to such strange behavior in the first place.

Whether it was a conscious thought, or the side effect of vain narcissism I do believe that in the eyes of my friends I stood somewhat atop that same pedestal I had placed my brothers upon all those years prior. And so I expected Kenny to be a bit thrown back by this unexpected revelation. I wasn't ready to hear him cry though. This thing in my heart cracked open and what poured from it was some cosmos of clustered emotion my body could only combat with tears. My coming out threw many people who loved me into this same abyss of confusion where I had been the lone resident for far too long, clawing for logic in a frantic seizure of compulsive gripping for anything that feels recognizable. The source of the man's tears was brotherly love manifest there in its purest form. It's madness, yes. But they're right when they tell you there are moments in a transition that you could never expect. They will transcend all measures of traditional human conveyance. And you'll only know someone has experienced something similar by this light that shines perpetually from the eye regardless of lot or status. Be you bum or baron, this mystical experience never extinguishes from a glint in the eye.

CHAPTER 19

THE RIG AND
THE *MALOOCH*

Regulators. Mount up. It's five thirty a.m., and that means two cups of strong brew and Warren G bumping in the gas station as I sit on the top of my utility boxes fueling my welding machine with diesel to start the day. It's a sweet and savory aroma I can no longer detect by traditional olfactory processes but rather taste through metaphorical means as this carbon-fueled ozone-boring monstrosity on wheels I sit upon converts labor, knowledge, and the sacrifice of one's physical wellbeing into cold, hard, diminishing-in-value U.S. banknotes. And in that sweet palm print of orange dawn, the song of blackbirds scraped to death over Maria Menounos's *Gas Station TV* advert suggesting that "we should take things as they come as sponsored by Dawn Dish Soap," and I can't help but think that maybe something has gone colossally wrong.

"It's gonna be a hot one. As heatwaves hit record highs across the country..." She screams this at me from the pump speaker, as I try to holster the diesel gas nozzle back into its receiver without rocketing the thing in uppercut fashion straight through the screen and her casual white T-shirt, which she looks fucking great in, *bitch*. My jaw finds that trench line sawed into my upper teeth back from the cokehead days and tightens until my teeth are perfectly socketed in that enamel groove. Consciously or unconsciously, I pluck the front of my oversized shirt away from the skintight Under Armor tank top and seamless bra hidden below that and get a little air movement against my skin to keep at bay the eventual adhesion of it all into one sweat-logged papier-mâché hauberk of cloth and my body's expelled minerals.

I buy two Gatorades and a bag of ice and load the cooler with lunch and fluids and bandanas and hats, so that at the height of the day's hell I can cut some of that stagnant heat that forms in an oven cut into the Earth ten feet down cooking my body in the enchilada wrappings of a fire-resistant Nomex jumpsuit of streetwear traffic cone complexion and a cowhide leather overcoat to protect my belly and arms from any further excessive spatter burns. An ice-loaded cap designed for dreadlock containment keeps my hair bundled up closer to my head, so I'm not pulling as many burnt fistfuls of black hair out of my shampooed skull every evening, and the ice lays right against the rear of my jugular providing a decent amount of heat reduction at that pinnacle temperature. All that, bundled together with the fact that spironolactone gives me orthostatic hypotension in the summer and so every time I stand after welding the underside of a pipe, which is every fifteen minutes on the fifteen minutes all day long, my blood pressure drops a solid twenty to forty points, and I nearly pass out on my feet.

Then there's my partner, a Plumple-stiltskin baby-faced fuzzball fattened on Daddy's titty milk and spoon-fed every high-paying Sunday and premier location since he budded from his father's mass of sea-sponge shape shortly before I got into the local. On a better day I actually liked the dude, but he'd launched into a tirade the day before, after I mentioned I took my actual brothers-in-law out for dinner who just so happen to be gay, and I suppose the thought of them eating food in public triggered his hatred for things *faggot*. He mentioned how his cousin was a *fat faggot,* and did well for himself financially, and he hated that fact, as though it was testament to America's decline, and that the lives of homosexuals should be relegated to the status of pauper at least from his point of view. In hindsight of it all, I sort of feel bad for the man-baby, as maybe there's a little trapped Ewok sashaying under his pic-a-nic basket-stealing exterior. That all of his armaments and defensive barriers look much more like the slave regiment of someone forced to wear Daddy's boots, and from the right vantage point with the right eye it looks more like a billboard than a barricade.

But I wasn't in the light then. I was barreling beyond the event horizon in some abysmal darkness lit up only from the current that passed between rage and insanity. And what I saw in those tortures were monsters made of my own vision, and I fought like a fool through it all combating hate with madness. And so Plumpy lived in my mind rent-free, as they say. And sawed fresh grooves into my teeth at the gas pumps in the mornings.

Financially, since I *broke out* with my rig and established myself as a gas distribution rig welder, it had been a profitable year. However, my supplemental regimen of a solid ounce per week of high-potency hash and edibles had burned up a lot of that extra cashflow. But it was keeping me from putting a bullet through my head, so I figured it was necessary at the time. It also bore a great psychological load as my truck doubled as a mobile chem lab in the event of a random drug test, which could be frequent depending on how "random" the computer-generated picks really were. All the while, God-forbid you pop through welding on live gas and create a vortex of fire spewing out at ninety psi that'll melt your face off pretty quick and leave them dissolving your ash and excrement in a ten panel that prevents your wife and children from collecting on the workman's comp. *But I'm a cowboy, on a steel rig I ride, and I'm wanted, dead or alive*, as a good friend of mine and fellow rig welder would sing all too often as he too dealt in matters of dirt and insanity.

I was losing it. It was too much stress. I was snapping out worse than in the cokehead days; verbal altercations with supervision, throwing buckets of rod, all the jerkoff things. I was becoming what I hated the most in this business. A jitbag. A know-it-all jitbag with a monkey on their shoulder, shit attitude, and disorder of the mood-swing variety. Worst yet, I wasn't even consistent. I could take a steady jerkoff as anyone can, but amiable one second and lunatic next, puts everyone on edge and sucks aggression and negativity to you like a great cosmic magnet. So, I get *jammed up.* A legal battle ensues, and it all feels like bad luck. I'd go into it more, but that battle may or may not still be ongoing at the time of this book's publication, and so forgive me for leaving it vague. No good deed goes unpunished, I would say. But in some unconscious realm, had I not willed it this way? I knew somewhere deep down, at least at that time, these two worlds could not cohabit, and so my transition attempt was destroying my working world. Exactly as I had prophesied.

They laid me off. So I took the next thing I could find, as I didn't know how my family could survive with cashflow so tightly strangulated. But Shelly found a way, as she always does, and I found myself in the underground steam tunnels of an elaborate gardens complex, laying the lines that would pump to a faux moat of some futuristic glass castle, which was to serve as an arboretum. It was actually a pretty interesting job, but I was dead above the neck. Having been honed with speed and precision from my time running gas pipe, I don't think my building trades brothers had seen someone weld as fast as me. So, I kept headphones plugged into my ears all day long, spoke to no one, and ripped weld after weld out over eight-hour days that would drag worse than fourteens. Although nothing was happening in the form of breast development at this point in my transition, I was convinced everyone on the job knew, and it scrambled me head to toe. I wore an extra baggy hi-vis vest and a chip on my shoulder visible from Earth's orbit. Every night I would cry on the bathroom floor, then I would step outside, smoke a blunt, and numb myself until the next day. That was every day, all the time, until I cracked again.

"Fuck it," she says. "Pull the money and write." I'm still half werewolf in this memory as the light of the moon maybe only pulled behind a passing cloud, but I hear her, I hear my wife speak to me with a confidence and clarity so strong it split the static of my mind's corroded conduits. She was speaking of the annuity I accrued since my time in the fitters. I was on the bathroom floor. I was naked, my face purple with stress and sorrow.

"Who cares. If it all fails, it fails. But I won't lose you. If you leave me…" She's fighting back every emotion that runs red in the face of flushed victims. "...I'll never forgive you." She says it through clenched teeth, and the blue fire of fallen seraphim. And there, my dear reader, is the vacuum of hell. That your own weakness breeds despair in the ever hopeful. I will not let that angel lose hope. And I won't lie and say I was hocked headlong out of this black hole and into a new horizon at that moment, squeezed from the sphincter of self-hate like some impacted nugget needing dislodgement. But I found some fizzle there in massless dark. She was losing her faith in the Lord, and I couldn't have that. I clung to a hope that I could restore her faith in things magnificent. Delusion, narcissism, madness, all valid conclusions, my keen analyst. But that is what I chose then and now forever.

So I *drug* the job. That means quit. And pulled a third of my annuity and started writing this book. I write every day until the second month mounts and financial desperation causes me to travel to the other side of the state with the rig, live on the road for a real loser contractor, and ultimately drag that job as well from red flags amassing in such multitude it results in another legal battle. And so, yet again, I can't divulge this rotten tale, but rest assured, your arrogant narrator is somehow still standing in the end.

While *out there*, on the road, I would roll blunts and smoke in the designated section as allocated by the Holiday Inn and pray to God to protect me. And I hoped that He and She was enjoying the show. If nothing else I'd like to think I gave the Lord a ride, a show worth watching, and that feels like a justice of this life. And so, the Good Lord, and the Dao, and the saints of all good faiths kept up their side of the prayer and I skated a drug test, four weld tests, and a jobsite that wanted me dead. Most importantly, at this peak period of uncertainty, on one lone stroll, thumbing the ash from a Philly, I heard a truth I could not deny. I was not a woman. It was not my experience of life. I never much had doors held open for me. I never got by on a wink and smile (eh, maybe I did.) But I didn't know what it felt like to hold the potentiality of pregnancy. I knew of sex only from the perspective of possessing a phallus. I inherited my family's genetic lack of finesse, and did not have much of that feminine flow that drives armies to war or names to be etched upon the strand in futile infatuation. But despite my lacking my mind's weak generalities of being *woman*, I could say, at that moment, with a fair degree of certainty, that I was this *other thing*. Possessing elements of both, but not limited by the definition of one. And in a mind at a time that was raging like a vortex, that felt like Truth. And I needed that, then and there.

A rickety six months passes. I get sober. Sober, sober. No weed, no bullshit, no nothing. I get insomnia. And the rage that comes with it. I take a job at a school over the winter, and on the first day my new boss tells me about this *freak* he met on his last job. His word, not mine. Not anymore.

"So I see this big motherfucker, right?" He begins his yarn, and me and the man-boy apprentice smile as seems warranted by the tone of his telling it.

"Big, ugly motherfucker. And I says to him, 'What do they call you, big fella?' And you know what he says? Susan!" I push my lower jaw into the sidewall of my mouth, my teeth still lipped up like a chimp at the zoo. The apprentice holds his sides in the excessive laughter of a developing blowjob.

"Can you believe that? A transgender. In this business? Can you imagine the fucking hell that guy goes through on a job?" The irony of the statement actually makes me laugh but not in the way he thinks. And to the audience of no one but myself I play along.

"I'm sure it's a living hell!" I say in comedic singsong. And the three of us laugh, all for different reasons.

That afternoon I have an appointment with my endocrinologist, and I tell her I'm suicidal. The worst I've ever been. I tell her I don't believe it's the transition but the world I'm in. All logic keeps indicating to me that once my career knows of my true identity, it will be mostly over.

She says, "Why don't you get a different job?"

And I say, "Why don't you go be a fucking foot doctor?"

She tries not to roll her eyes, then I remind her, "Not for nothing, doc, but I might make more than you do." That's a bluff but these white-collar fucks don't know that, and I'm sure there's a contractor or two living in her gated community she can't quite put her finger on and so fuck it, I fired the shot across the bow. Plus, it's a spot of aggravation amongst welders of a premier quality, like it didn't take us as long or longer than med school to hone our skills to the level required to do what it is we do.

She bows her head and says, "You might."

Then I ask her if I have to keep injecting myself with these turkey baster needles she ordered for me, and she says, "No," and "Why are you using needles so big?"

I remind her that she ordered them for me.

After the appointment I read her summary notes. "Work a little stressful, but otherwise doing well." My estrogen level was over nine hundred units (which is stupid high) and I said I was going to kill myself. I dusted her then and there.

In the shower I called out to God, yet again, and just said, "Help me." And the ever-timely Almighty answered, as They always did, answering every one of my prayers that really mattered.

That week I start working out again. Meditation and my studies of the Zen way ate up some of the greater rage-filled pie slice that was my emotional mind. And we find a new doctor. A down-to-earth nurse practitioner who just so happens to be a transwoman. Feeling her understanding that I wasn't completely insane was a great healing that felt near immediate.

"You should have told her to go be a podiatrist!" she says in response to my endocrinologist story. I try not to say "I love you," in response. She orders me bearable needles, she regulates my dosage to a rational level, and she just talks with me for a minute. Someone who knows. That helps a great deal.

--- - --- - --- - --- - --- - --- - --- - --- - --- - --- - --- - --- - --- - --- - --- - --- - --- - --- - ---

During this time my parents moved again. Dad had just finished renovating a home back in the Poconos at seventy-two years old. Then they got a dog, then they got rid of the dog. Then a toilet went bad and flooded some carpeting in the master bedroom. Between the toilet, the ruined vanity, and replacing the bedroom rug, all of it cost maybe a couple grand. But whatever false notion of peace that had taken shape in their mind was sullied by the disruption. Dad had an obsessive-compulsive breakdown. Over some toilet water. This happened once several years ago, and it took months and a home renovation to snap him out of it. And Mom likely thought that old sled dog might have one good drive left in him. My father, the only dog she ever kept, was the excuse of many moves and her only means of ever pulling off a single one.

"It's a fifty-five and older in Jersey, near the shore, won't the kids love that?" she says.

"Listen, I don't care what you do," I tell her.

"I know you don't care, Chuckie."

"Not like that, Ma. I mean I don't judge anything you do. Who the hell am I? What do I know?"

"I think my dad is trying to get me back to Cape May," she says of her deceased father.

"Maybe. Why Jersey? Dad hates liberals, crowds, traffic, gun reform, and flat land. That's basically the state in a nutshell."

"Yeah, but the beach. And he can ride his bike on the boardwalk. And I'm gonna get walking and get a bike. I think it's going to get me in good shape."

"Mom, let me explain the full reality of the Jersey Shore to you. The summers are fun enough if you like that. But in the fall when the normal mass of society returns to their working life back in the cities, it's nothing but old people and drug addicts left behind to weather out the winter together. And why a fifty-five and older?"

"Because we're old, Chuck!" Just a nip. Not the full snap, but she's nipping now.

"Yeah, but you did this before. Bent Pine?" I try to remind her of a former property back when I was about eighteen.

"Where?"

"Bent Pine. You purchased a fifty-five and older trailer park home on Bent Pine, then had a panic attack when you realized you didn't really own the land underneath, or that the lot fees would slowly bleed you dry for the rest of your life. And isn't the loan something weird? Like it's not a traditional mortgage or something?"

"But they have a pool."

"Bent Pine had a fucking pool!"

"Yeah, but this one's indoor."

"Oh, Jesus Christ. Listen, I'll give you my opinion as you give me yours. I don't think you should make this move. One thousand percent, I don't think you should make this move. But I support whatever decision you make. And who the fuck am I?"

By the time of this conversation, their house was already on the market and an offer placed on this fifty-five and older in Jersey. The move happened in the background of all of our lives, and it's sort of sad that my brothers and I didn't even crack jokes about it anymore. That the addiction of perpetual motion exhausted the threshold of retelling or even belittling, and we all just shrugged like it must just be that boy on the hill again, crying wolf.

They moved and I took a job in a shop for about a week before the rig work picked back up. There we jammed Neo-Soul tracks through a small speaker stuffed into a pipe end for amplified acoustics with another music lover and I ripped out lo-hi caps on a positioner that made the men salivate in their symmetry. Then one strange Thursday night, I was to take an old friend out for dinner in the city. He had run away years ago because he burnt a mob booky for twenty or thirty grand, but now he was back concerning an old court case and an assault. He was suing the guys who kicked his ass years ago. And I'd bet my house he started the whole damn thing. His name was Jerry Kim, one of my best friends from an old life lived, and I was saddened to learn he might have become a great hypocrite.

I picked him up in the hood after work. I was dressed as a male.

"Minivan...Bro, you're driving a minivan..." he said.

"What are you talking about? It's an SUV."

Then he pulls a bag of coke out right there in my passenger seat.

"The fuck are you doing?" I ask him. "There's baby seats and kid shit in here."

"Chill, bra." And I can tell he's been jazzed all day.

"I haven't seen you in five fucking years and you're already pissing me off. I can't be around this shit no more. Do it in the bathroom when we get there, you fucking animal."

He rolls his eyes and says, "Fine."

After the food, he tells me to stop at his friend's house for a minute for a house party. He can tell I'm hesitant and so cites reference to a few members of that old crew we had there, back in the bad days, and I choke up on my grip of the steering wheel nervous of exactly how the *old crew* has fared these last five years.

"Keiran!" It's Hwa-Young, and I haven't seen her since that time on the mountain when she told me she likes Hentai porn and that she was single. I think at the time my response was, "Rad." Then we sat silently on the car ride home through a blizzard, she entirely confused as to why we weren't making out after this intimate disclosure. She squeezes me tight with numbed up coke strength. Then I look around and realize the whole room has been ripping gaggers for hours now and we are well on our way to a full themed eighties party this most wretched of Thursday nights.

"Get me out of here," I whisper to no one or maybe myself.

Then I see a phone call from my mom, which is weird because it's ten o'clock at night.

"Chuckie!? Chuckie!" My mother is frantic. And she is sobbing.

"What?!" The whole room looks at me knowing full well the tone of voice of a bad phone call.

"I broke my shoulder, and they fucking robbed us! Dad's going nuts!" She says all this through sobs.

"What!?"

She had slipped on the boardwalk earlier in the day, landing straight on her right shoulder and shattering the ball joint there in its socket. While at the hospital, somebody broke into their new place at the fifty-five and older. They stole a butcher knife, some of my father's documents, and all of his handguns. I eyed Kim right then and there and thought, "Nahhh, he's been with me the whole time."

I'm not sure if I even said goodbye. I just put my shoes on and left, went home, grabbed the shotgun, and headed across the bridge and into that damnable state, New Jersey. I called my brother Mitch on the ride.

"Dad sounds like a Chihuahua ate a bag of meth," he tells me, and I laugh.

"I'll try to calm him down," I tell him.

Then he goes, "It wasn't you, right?"

"It wasn't me what?" I say back. And then he just says nothing and good luck.

I feed my dad a couple Ativan and force him to sleep. Then I sit up all night on the couch with the shotgun beside me and flinch against every creak and whistle that comes from outside the house.

A few weeks pass, and she says it all feels like the Malooch. I swallow three *I told you so's* right then and there.

And then I say, "I don't know, maybe." And she makes this very sad sound.

"Ah, life's too wild to know, Mom. Maybe if you stayed up there in the woods, the bear would have got you, and I'd be sifting diamond earrings out of bear shit right now."

"That was the first time we all spent under the same roof together in a long time. Just the three of us," she said. "That was nice, right?"

"Yeah, it was nice, Mom."

They moved about a month or two later, back to the same town in the mountains they had just come from. And questioned me often as to why someone would want to complicate their life with a gender transition. That it was just out of the wheelhouse of their understanding, and that I was making a terrible mistake.

--- - --- - --- - --- - --- - --- - --- - --- - --- - --- - --- - --- - --- - --- - --- - --- - --- - --- - ---

So now I'm back with the rig. A couple threatened lawsuits, a couple mental breakdowns, and a couple brushes with suicide, and I'm back with the rig. Right where I started when I started this book. Black hairs spring from me in places they never appeared before, and I attribute it to the testosterone-driven workday of this world. It is the sunup to sundown days of rig welder existence. We take a lunch break now, which is atypical on this side, but only because the contractor wants to nickel and dime us on time, so we play the game. Other than that, it is full bore, heavy hustle pipe slinging, that at the least runs just slightly ahead of your galloping self-destructive mental dialogue. But deadlifting pipe, manhandling nine-inch grinders, working oversized birdcages, swinging six-pound mauls, rigging, climbing, rolling, slanging, all of it like a defibrillator pad attached right to your deadened testicles, juicing whatever anabolic fluids can be mustered from the relic appendages. And so maybe that's where this inner turmoil bubbles out of. The chemical consequence of a body put under extreme and generally masculine conditions.

Maybe it's just frustration. Logic broad-face bashing the manic sprinter just as she rounds the corner of her maypole flourish. Thoughts like, "What's the point?" shatter the twig reinforcement of my mostly sand-based foundation, and I feel like I can't even imagine a world where the female version of me exists. These are hard days. These are limbo days. I hang on out of pure instinct in a lightless tunnel with no end in sight.

CHAPTER 20

HEAVEN IS A BIG, BIG SWING

Electrolysis hurts. I make it nine minutes. Then I tell her I need a pause. Then she zaps free one more hair and I bug. "I'm good," I tell her. "I'll pay you for the full time, but I'm not... I'm not in the right headspace for this right now." I don't like needles. And, well, it's been one of those days. Five hours ago, my ankle was crushed between two 24" diameter pipes by a herky jerk operator too rammy to wait for my damn signal, and I'm sucking up that pain and willing away any potential fracture because I can't take another investigation on the system I'm working on or they'll never hire me back, and money's too damn tight right now. And an hour before all that, a phone call from supervision sends me down to the benzene saturated gas plant where the dirt runs black from chemical saturation, and I guess it all fucks with my head as one of my best friends from my apprenticeship class is on his fifth round of chemotherapy from similar exposure.

And so, it's the next day, and I'm off and it's the morning, and I'm noodling a guitar with four packs of ice wrapped around my foot when I feel it. For me it starts in the teeth, but like a bullet through the belly, it's the exit wound you need to worry about. Electric will. Fire rage. When the water that makes up most of your organic structure flashes instantly to steam, and the thermodynamic reaction through the body stiffens you head to toe. You ever feel it? A thrombosis of the pneumatic system of your pistons and tubing, it'll hammer through the turns of your body until it comes blasting out through your toes and your balled fists, and if some great bestial roar doesn't come out of you, then it's a mean, hard knuckle that forms in the throat where all sound throughout the whole universe gets swallowed down into the belly where it grumbles for all eternity. And you'll stand. You always stand at these moments. Broken foot, imbecile, or dead, it is the reanimator of lifeless, stupid things. The great defiler of sanctimonious logic. The loogy in the face of lethargy. That beautiful infinite manifestation of, "Fuck you, what else you got!"

I gotta say, the fifteen hairs she pulled look pretty damn smooth in the harsh light of day. And so I call her back up and schedule an hour for the following week. And I try again.

That night I put my son to bed, and he tells me about this dream he had. "Da, Da, Dad, hey, Dad?"

"Yeah, bud?"

He just turned three the day before.

"I had a dream, there was a, uh, uh, big, big swing. Sooo big," And he spans his arms as wide as they'll reach. "We all sit on it, and swing so high. So, so high." He gives me a hug and there's water forming in my eyes.

"I have the same dream, buddy." And he lays down and closes his eyes.

What a blessing. To live eternal in the dreams of our children. Heaven is a big, big swing, and it swings sooo high.

CHAPTER 21

CHEMICAL ZEN

There is some cord that runs the length of me. And in the night, tethered to my heels and the back of my skull, dry air drives a rot through my already shriveled sleeping coil and causes a brittle sort of tear stimulating enough to pulley wide my loosely clasped eyelids and raise the curtain against soundless dream overture like the signaled huff of an orchestra's extinguished tuning. And to the off-tempo beat of some amateurish mental stage director, the monologue of monkey chatter resumes from the previous evening's ever diminishing ramble. But with this particular black dawn, there is no accompanying cold sweat, palpitations of the anxious heart, or schemes of vengeance against unborn future infractions. There is only cold clarity. A blissfully insane sort of delusion that blankets the greater madness and chokes from it the fuel of its fiery ignition. Maybe a middle way. I've coined it a Zen of the chemical age. A stubble faced, tiny-titted, throaty sort of *Aum* that opens to the many opinions of life properly lived, but clings to none of it. And all of *that*, impossibly translatable back into a semantic digestion of logical language, all the while knowing its dreamy comprehension is fleeting like the taste of salty slobber particalized onto the tongue by a mop-wrung dog, and it's more the notion of its occurring that stays with you rather than remememberable, classifiable taste. But in futility, I'll attempt a proper cracking of this codex of infinite simplicity, and present to you, hopefully, a less infuriating, more matter-of-fact explanation of this strange morning lucidity that might be nothing more than smokestack smog settling as misinterpreted mountain mist. Perhaps this is why Christ and gurus alike speak mostly in parable, as glimpses of concepts divine just sound stupid in the language of those you are trying to enlighten.

Not to claim I know or possess the characteristics required of a no bullshit bodhisattva, because I most certainly do not, but I'm seeing things differently for the first time in my life, and even if I'm dead wrong, which I usually am, then it is a duty to *you,* my potential reader, that this celestial injustice be recorded as nothing more than a *DO NOT ENTER* sign of cardboard construction, that you can choose to either heed or ignore depending on your disposition at the time of your reading it. But as always, before all that, there's this...

I have one tattoo on my body. Changes permanent have always frightened me. And so I bind my budding breasts to my chest with formfitting layers and still roll around in the night, swatted this way and that like some waterlogged, low inertia tennis ball that only properly serves the game once all the wet has been fully racketed from it. Tonight's match is on whether or not I should eliminate the hair on my face. What funny things we are, us madmen. That at the midpoint of change logic tells us to retrace our steps, that the retreat of needle and scalpel is now seemingly more acceptable than just floating downriver atop the debris of this dam I destroyed and seeing what larger bodies await me further downstream. That I would be more content in what is known rather than what is unknown. Teenage me would slap the shit out of me right now. But then again, he didn't know much of the lash of the perpetual whip and its consequence of occasional hesitation.

There's a coward in my mind. It comes in the mornings, and it comes at night. It talks to me in the car sometimes. It says things like *what,* and *why,* and *how.* I want to kill it, but it will probably never go away. I drug it sometimes with Ativan and then it sleeps with me. And takes me to strange, long-existing dream worlds where reunions of past souls meet for judgement and acceptance alike. And then I wake and drag the groggy coward to the toilet and hear it bellow and whine and pray to the Lord, not too loudly, to keep him at bay. Let him sleep. And give me a miracle.

I *need* another miracle. If I get coffee in me quick enough, maybe we can leave the geek back in the dirt, where surely he'll find us days later by the scent of our campsite and whine in that perfect frequency that cracks the welds of gussets and shakes the structures of steel that lives try to be built upon. But we can get a few days' head start. Put a couple smiles into the memories of these children and feel in all of its beautiful delusion that miracles manifested of our own blanket insanity are maybe almost possible against the rabble of a world that says it isn't.

Oh, and don't forget there's hellfire waiting for you when you fail. Those moments feel like real courage when the coward's sleeping. Eternal damnation pitted against a good-looking pair of skinny jeans and some slightly less elongated vocal folds. Spin the wheel, drop the ball, roll the dice. I'll take the long shot on a green sky tomorrow, not for payout, but for that brief staticky look upon your face trying to buffer a reality that didn't download correctly. And when I'm wrong, you're welcome for that contented feeling warming your gut right now, that the things you know to be true are, and I'm sorry to that child in you that held its breath for that brief interval between dawn's orange and the ocean of blue it outruns all day long.

So, what's the coward whining about this time? Well, they don't recommend laser for my face. A life of dusk till dawn sun exposure with the additional seasoning of perpetual UV exposure as a result of a welder's primary function, likely infuses my skin with an excess of melanin so laser treatments could potentially burn me, targeting my beautiful wrinkling epidermis rather than the fly-like black filaments that bespeckle it. Which, if administered incorrectly or without caution could create a mostly permanent, scale-like, lizard-skinned burn pattern, which isn't entirely what I'm going for with this rockabilly/surfer chick look I'm trying to feebly muster. (Alas, some Christian sects could rest easier having visibly confirmed my demonic or Reptilian influence and one-way ticket to the great AC/DC concert in the ground, but I digress.)

So I book two electrolysis appointments and walk away from both consultations a little shaky that again exposure to high quantities of UV radiation and daily face washes of microscopic metal dust powdering the freshly zapped openings of my hair extracted pores has never been encountered before by the two most reputable electrologists of my area. And I think, "Well, dangit. Work just picked up and I'm back with my rig. So now what?"

I pray to the Lord for a lottery win. Nothing big. Just enough to take off work for six months. Finish my book. Zap my face for a while. And fully attack this other career path I'm trying to manifest out of thin air. But in the morning, with five measly numbers shy of a million dollars, I realize I wouldn't want it even if I could manifest it. The path is making something out of nothing. Against all odds. This is my archery. My swordsmanship. This is the path of my unfettered mind. It's pretty much the same Zen philosophy, just with more lace. But the same lack of hesitation is equally required. So, let's talk about that now, while I'm in some mindset to do it. This new notion of Zen. Same as the old. A one for the chemical age.

I have one tattoo on my body. It is an image of Bodhidharma in the form of a daruma doll with one eyelid missing and no bullshit expression of bliss on his face. His teeth are biting through his lip, and if he sees enlightenment he sees it only half at the snapshot of that image, and watches tea leaves sprout from the discarded shmuck of his fileted lid skin. It's a cute enough faerie story of tea's inception and its acceptance into the culture and way of Zen. An acceptable drug of the Way, on that path of enlightenment, to beat back sleep that crowds the determined practitioner like Publisher's Clearing House just trying to deliver the fucking check.

There's not too much talk of transgenderism in the lakes of religion I've paddled through in the course of my life. I've tried to find an acceptable answer there, but I haven't. Changing one's gender and the lifestyle of the Zen abject seem to be two entirely contradictory things, and thus may be a proper koan for a life of consistent weirdness. By all logic, attachment to my physical form, be it male, female, or something in between is a pretty nuts and bolts torque pattern to the path of grand delusion by the least confusing of Buddhist ground rules. Certainly, weekly injections into the subcutaneous fat of my lower abdomen with an unnaturally "opposite" bodily hormone must go against all notions of *flow*, whatever that bullshit has evolved into and maybe has always been. But I'm real good at sniffing out bullshit, both the good and the bad. Ironically, I have no actual sense of smell from a lifestyle of tooted powder, but my ability to sense hypocrisy and horseshit is near superhuman, maybe for no other reason than I'm bulging with it myself. And so I think of the tale of Bodhidharma and the birth of the tea leaf; a caffeine-induced, buzzcutted bliss regime that rings of the smallest pulse of attachment even if that attachment is to the Way. And then I think of the Lord on the Cross, and think there it is in a nutshell, and maybe if the red-eyed sage could blink every now and again we'd catch the occasional flinch that living in this world brings even to the enlightened.

Nobody knows anything about Jesus Christ from the ages of thirteen to thirty. History dorks speculate, as is their job, but nobody knows for sure. I'd like to think maybe he was out there fucking up. Hanging with whores, and pulling pinot up by the bucketful from every well he dipped his holy hand into. And then, maybe something happened. I don't know what. A prolonged fast, a meeting at the crossroads, maybe a fiddle showdown with the prince of darkness. I wasn't there, and I don't know hell about history, so I won't speculate. But maybe the man awoke, and became the God we know him as, and weaved life and death and sickness and blindness as easily as a fabric turning over and revealing its other side. And like the revelation of a good high or a good dream, he knew all, most of the time, and went with his *flow* until it found him on a cross choking to death, with his belly stabbed, crying out to the celestial Father, "My God! My God! Why have you deserted me?"

And I think, *Yes! There it is!* That the delusion of life was even too convincing for the Son of God at its pinnacle agony, and so just for a moment, fell into the role of a man dying on a cross instead of a God ascending to his heavenly throne. But the glory of enlightened beings is that their intervals of delusion are shorter than ours, and with a choke and gasp he remembers,

remembers who he really is, the God that is us all. And sees Himself playing the very role that is crucifying Him. Sees Himself in the dying men next to Him, one a believer, one not. Sees Himself in the tears of women, and the jeers of gambling soldiers. Yes, then he remembers. "Father, forgive them, for they do not know what they are doing."

The parts we play are convincing things. Whatever you are, gender nonconforming hopeful or binary righteous, can you break the role for just a moment and temporarily blind yourself to the light of all opinions? But what the hell do I know? I'm just the bobbing apple in the unpunctured bucket of bolts rusted in rainwater or the scrunched up one in the larynx of choked throats, sometimes the one with the worm through it and sometimes the unplucked one in the tree on the lot near my childhood house. But most of the time I'm the voice that looks back at that sentence and says, "What the fuck does that mean?"

Well, if there's one thing I've uncovered through all *this*: a transition is a surefire way to corkscrew an ego extraction right through the side of your temple. Just be careful with that ripely hollowed out orifice because I see a lot of trans folk mushing a malformed fresh one right back into the cavity with all the same pitfalls and pities of an overly attached ego. Not to tell you to not play the part. I think that's sort of the point too. Be the girl, the boy, the thing or non-thing you want to be; just tread lightly, or find yourself in a role with a whole new cast of villains that need slaying. Maybe it's getting muddled, this explanation. So, allow me to speak for myself and no one else, and if you take something from it, good, and if you're offended by it, good: that's your "X." There's a treasure underneath that spot. Start digging there.

I don't like my facial hair anymore. Hairs on my belly grow like the hairs of Seth Brundle after his DNA was fused with that of a common housefly. After a day in the slag pits, grime coats the lines in my face in masculinizing ways that no amount of estrogen will possibly reverse. My biggest fear in taking this leap of faith into transitioning my gender was becoming what my mind derogatorily coined, The Titty Man. A hairy boob-ed, masculine creature, baritone in voice and demeanor, with neither the time nor energy to even fake femininity in its slightest. And yet, at the halfway point, isn't that what I am right now? In the eternity of NOW, I am my deepest fear. And yet, Jack Daniel's doesn't slosh around my belly, copper-jacketed teardrops of lead remain outside the perimeter of my skull, ropes of eight twists rest in uncoiled piles, and my head still bounces off the concrete floor instead of rocketing through it. Should I succeed, in all of that in which I wish to succeed: a smooth skinned, velvet voiced vampiress femininely passable in both mind and body? And should I feel that unknown feeling, which I set out to achieve many years before now, if only for just one flickering moment? And then the bombs drop? Or the trans are rounded up by the trainload and gassed in chambers ironically clad in my Lord of the Cross? Or hormones are made extinct and all my work retracted, the dam of temporary femininity sundered, and rotten masculine flow allowed to reengage? What then? Is it okay then to sip my whiskey, and spin my pistol, and burn at high noon, the vampiress and the Titty Man? That answer is no. The answer is stay open to all options, but cling to none of it. Gorgeous or gargantuan, the courage of your living is what the world needs more than anything. Hated, loved, or crucified, you have a purpose in the mind of God. So be the carrot-colored monks of uninspired hairdo, or the coffin-tipped vixen of your wildest dreams; be the high and tight conservative of traditional family values, or screw in piles like dogs. All of it is under the stage direction of the Almighty. Your greatest virtue, completely blind of Enlightenment, as I am now and likely will be always, is to respect the part of the actor adjacent, be open to the spittle of their beating violence and humble yourself to the judgements of their despair and their greatest wishes, for these too are the tattooed knuckles of that thing called Dao.

CHAPTER 22

SHIT AGAINST THE WALL

The violence of the fray, the chop and churn of white water, the bob and buoy of breath in rhythm against it all, and you there, a twig paddling, happy enough for those glassy intervals between groundswell and break where the ocean isn't actively shattering you against the shoreline. And then one day, you make it. Just past the breakers, into the lineup and beyond. A far, flat sea and with it, the unknown mysteries of what's below and what's before you. No new landmass forms on the horizon, and the one you just fought so hard to free yourself from shrinks there behind you. I've determined it's much scarier here, past the breakers, out in the currentless sea, where your survival and sanity are entirely dependent on correct instinct or lucky guess.

I never thought I'd get this far. Hell, with any of it. Fitting, welding, transitioning, sobriety, writing, and then all this shit I threw against the wall. I figured I would have long since doubled back by now. Finally satisfied with the slurry of shit that was the life I left, now knowing for sure that my half-realized dreams are far more hellish than anything abandoned back in my *old* life, which is a failure in vernacular because it's the same life as my *new* one. Then one day, just ready to turn back, you see some strange glint from out the sea, like maybe some Atlantean scout had your scalp the whole time, right in her reticule ready to pull the trigger at a hair's whisper. But it's only the mirage of the marooned, and as you come upon that sparkling trinket, you find it is a bottle with a cork and a message inside. Written on it says

Keep going, stupid. And it's in your handwriting, and you don't even remember tossing it into the sea.

Maybe now you'll make that future coast. And after you burn the proverbial boats, as they say, and storm the shores like a Viking ready to seize it all or die trying, and fail in that first onslaught, and stand again now with your back to the waves, weaponless and bleeding, you may devolve in those moments into something between ape and *Australopithecus*, and sling shit shat straight into your open palm forward and into the faces of those who press you back into the sea you just came from. And when you get one, right in the eyes, and see flinch that which so had you dead to rights a second ago, then you might feel it. Some latent DNA synapse firing, an entirely animal roar will rattle the network of all human evolution and come ripping out of your throat, ready to take what's yours with nothing more than your damn mitts if need be. And you might just realize it was your weapons and armaments slowing you down this whole time.

As I was trying to leave a career I loved to let blossom an identity whose form I could not even imagine, I started plastering The Wall with every turd formed enough to fling. One day, I bought a pack of Micron pens and a small inventor's logbook, and spent the very early turmoil of my transition smoking weed on my back porch and drawing inventions into the book. Then one day something formed. I drew something in my log that when I showed it to people their eyes widened. I've been fortunate enough to see the look before in a couple lines of scribbled prose or a slick weld cap in a tough spot. That look reads as *We have something here.*

So I hired a patent attorney. I was broke, mind you, but at the time I did it as nothing more than an educational experience, a college course if you will in the creation of a patent, and I figured if I did it once I would never have to hire an attorney again, or so I surmised at the time. My attorney was an old marathon man, just like myself, and he's likely the smartest human being I've ever met in the living flesh thus far in my life, and so let's call him Bubba, as that's about the most opposite moniker I can think for the man. Not to say Bubbas can't be brilliant, and maybe I only use the name because a transwoman who didn't even know she was a guide in my life used to go by it, and she just blew her brains out in the street last week because some ratfuck outed her in the conservative Baptist town where Bubba was mayor and pastor, and where Britanni was forced to peek from the shadows.

But I digress. There, in attorney Bubba's office, in my skinny jeans and white Gap women's T-shirt, pink shoelaced sneaks, and a leather jacket that stopped at my midriff, Bubba didn't even blink at any of that, and saw only the ink on my pages. There we sat for several hours, scheming about ways to wall off this piece of intellectual property that even sent the old stoic slobbering some when he first digested the simplicity and applications of such a potential product.

As I awaited the issuance of my patent, I did not stay stagnant, and so was birthed TracWear, a one-sided electromagnetic frequency protective pouch for the purpose of housing a tracking device on the wearer's clothing without pumping an inordinate amount of radiation into the wearer, especially in the case of a child, while simultaneously allowing the device to communicate with its respective network. Michelle and I started an LLC. We turned a back room into a manufacturing facility, spent our nights learning the intricacies of ecommerce and EMF radiation, and even started shipping a few pairs of our patent-pending TracWear Children's Underwear to a handful of parents across the country who wanted to safely, securely and comfortably keep an eye on the most precious thing in their lives: their child.

This is what occupied the hours not steamfitting during my early transition. That and writing this book. All that annuity money I pulled went straight to my patent, my business, my book, electrolysis, laser hair removal, two pairs of shoes, and three mortgage payments, all in a desperate juggling act to find some way to the other side. Then one day in the basement, nothing manifesting, having freshly given my head a couple forceful dribbles against the concrete floor, I sat on the computer and sent in the most underhand pitched application to *Shark Tank* probably ever submitted. But I did it. And then forgot about it entirely.

Months dragged on and I churned through limbo. A semiformed halfling, mean as all hell by day and sweet as licorice after clock out, manic and mistreated, mixed up and alone, except for Michelle and my beautiful children, which of course is more than the whole world. Then we took a vacation with Michelle's family, and I was very, very, very low. Again, it was to God and in a bathroom, and I was pleading this time not for a final fix but just a sign. Just something to send my way to say, "All these *crazy* things you've been doing, I see them, and they're not as crazy as you think."

We were unpacking our bags after vacation. I was sitting on the toilet checking my emails when I read So and So from *Shark Tank* wanted to set up a phone interview to discuss my business TracWear. My kneejerk was somebody must be messing with me. Two days later, I walked out of my office having just finished an extensive phone interview with this *Shark Tank* producer from the email. Michelle stood on the porch with her hands over her mouth.

"Uh," I said. "We're semi-finalists for season fifteen of *Shark Tank.*"

"Shut up," she said.

"We beat out sixty thousand applicants. We made it to the top two hundred."

"Shut up!" she said.

"We're fucking semi-fucking-finalists for season fucking...!" And then she kissed me. Hardest damn kiss she ever gave me, but she kissed me.

And then in the bathroom, looking in the mirror at myself, today not in disgust, and I said to that image, and I said to the Lord, "Thank you! Dear God, thank you!"

Now, spoiler alert for all my would-be inventors and entrepreneurs out there, but if you make it that far in the process on the show, they give you a wicked assignment and only a short number of days to complete it. A catchy ten-minute pitch video and a mountain of paperwork as extensive or more so than a full business plan, and there's no exceptions for late submission. I'd imagine it's structured to test the mettle of real entrepreneurs rather than the multitude of half-formed ones submitted like somebody's going to finish the work for you. Which one was I?

I was about to find out.

For a year and a half, I had felt flip-flopped. Male, female, monkey, man, miscreant, monster, all of them mixed up and flung off centrifugally based on their density at that particular moment. But not now. Not when I was making that video. There and then, I was Rae in all her brilliance, shining for the world if for just one flicker of light. A few days after that small amount of *Shark Tank* validation, and I never felt so good in my transition. All of a sudden, there was a prototype for the future, if even it was just constructed in spider's silk. A plan to exercise, pass better, voice modification, and the necessity to gain confidence presenting as female in public before I'd be put on display in front of fifteen million viewers. One week to flimflam a *Shark Tank* pitch and a gender transition...shit, the universe was letting me off easy for once, knowing full well I could do it all in half the time. I thanked God with every free thought I had at that time.

We didn't get on the show. But I didn't detransition. And here I am, still writing, still shipping underwear, still scheming for some way to bring light into the dark, hollow spaces of the world. Look for the signs. The Universe is still sending them to you. But don't stop throwing shit against the wall, because even if it falls off a month later, that breath-held pause is a damn fine feeling in the interval of defied gravity. And best yet, you'll find you made it one month further than you thought you could ever go.

CHAPTER 23

TIME

It's the same sunrise everywhere. But there are places on this planet, ripples in the world's rind, atmospheric striations that rake the granular light apart into long, slender fingers only for the delicate beams to be shattered against the sea and sent across the world in shimmer sawcut from the sun's source. And in these particular places, particulate photons pool like palms of milk in the cradled interval of lapped wake against the shore. If one was conscious enough in these moments, one could wade out into the waters and skim the light right off the top of the sea glass. Keep it in an old mason jar with a screw-top lid, and save its illumination for only the most dire of rescue missions. Like when the light of fireflies fade. Or should you need to prove that magic exists.

My daughter's hair and overgrown lavender, stabbed as sprigs into the coast, catch the wind in the same updraft; locked, the two of them, in hypnotic revelry of that groggy orange dawn and the way that sleepy inlet tilt the sun in trajectories that could only be described as kaleidoscopic.

Everything feels like it's covered in sand. All of us in some grainy filter, some sandstorm snapshot of this amplified and damn near tangible feeling that this moment is completely and utterly finite. So much so I can almost roll the moments between my fingertips and feel them fall away from me into some untouchable place of the past. I will never again get my daughter in the dawn in pajamas, the sunlight silver sifted through her golden braids, youth at that age and that moment for all of us, the weight of my son in my arms; the crisp chill in muffled humidity that makes the air feel like something you could grasp between your hands and snap. Gone, a spectral snapshot shed just one second behind you forever and as light as a breath to your grasp. These moments, their delicacy, these places in particular proximity to this same sun everywhere, this all fires through the cerebral cortex like a real neural jumpstarting and brands pathways permanent into a new series circuit that sees the world just shy of extrasensory.

But it's getting cold. I'm getting hungry. I need a coffee. Let's go, hun.

And you stoop down, and you scoop up the kids, and you take one step out of that arbitrary perimeter that encapsulates these places of power and breathe deep the fog of life, forgetting almost all of what you just experienced. Except, of course, this thread that glints against the silhouette of your scrambling children and disappears just behind their next movement, or that light breeze, unnoticeable before a distinct lurch forward in the pace of the treadmill of life. But you know now, whether you say it aloud or not, that these moments too are pouring off of you like showers of sand. Disappearing faster than you could pool them up. It's the same sunrise everywhere.

And it is so in respect of this new reality. You waste time no more. There is no more hiding; the sand will find you there as well. But it should not be some somber realization. That you may be so blessed as to coat the shores of scenic coastal sunrises, what adventures will you hum into the heels of those who come to wade those future waters? That a grain of sand could hold in it the pinnacle singularity of an entire person's life and sit content, near invisible, semi-conscious, sleeping in the short intervals of the wave's curl, coating a shoreline snaking the eternity of all things forever happening. Then hinge shut your idiot jowls, because it is not then, it is now. And even then, when then is now, you may dream of now, when now *was* now, and so need either way to press on back into the thick folds of undulating ego, and in efforts both noble and futile, champion whatever missions and messages forward and out and right back into our own stupid face, until the next curl whistles from a wave tripping over a sandbar and stirs us awake from this dream we can barely remember. And the wave rolls back into the sea and it's the sound of the whole world's breathing, and you're back asleep and right where we left off, and it's just getting to the good part now.